The Poison Tree
Planted & Grown in Egypt

I0629963

Reflections on Relationships
Marwa Rakha

Marwa Rakha
The Poison Tree
Planted & Grown in Egypt
Reflections on Relationships

1st Edition: January 2008

2nd Edition: March 2008

3rd Edition: April 2009

4th Edition: July 2009

Dar Al-Kutub record number: 2008/2766
ISBN: 9780982080405

Illustrations By: Karim Terouz
Cover Design: Dalia William

Malamih Publishing House

El-Diwan Street, Garden City, Cairo, Egypt
Tel/Fax: +20227949885 - +20112771522
E-mail: editor-en@malamih.com
Website: http://malamih.com
Managing Director: Mohamed Elsharkawy

To everyone who contributed to my spiteful nature,
Those who nurtured my venom,
Those who were stung,
Those who survived,
And those who died!
To a society that unleashed my voice
While trying to smother me.
To the women of this society;
The universal Eve.
To men;
My greatest source of inspiration,
My only hope for liberation,
And my worst fear.
To you.

A tribute to William Blake

I was angry with my friend:
I told my wrath, my wrath did end.

I was angry with my foe:
I told it not, my wrath did grow.

And I water'd it in fears,
Night & morning with my tears;

And I sunned it with my smiles,
And with soft deceitful wiles.

And it grew both day and night,
Till it bore an apple bright;

And my foe beheld it shine,
And he knew that it was mine,

And into my garden stole
When the night had veil'd the pole:

In the morning glad I see
My foe outstretch'd beneath the tree

Once upon a time …

No

~~Once upon a time …~~

This is not the usual story that starts with once upon a time … It is a story that happens all the time … In Egypt.

A little girl of 19.

Dragging her feet between her parents; holding their hands as she walked heavily. The park was so crowded with children running up and down the green alleys. She could not run ... she never could ... she wished she could ... their grip was so tight ... if only she could.

An old soul in the body of a kid, she eyed the baby who had the face of an angel and a smile that warmed the soul. With pride and honor she took responsibility of the baby; to protect and to cherish; to dress and to nourish.

A silly girl of 21.

When no one was looking, she took the girl to the playground. On a huge step, she sat with the baby girl seated between her legs as she watched a game. Watching the muscular, well-built guys run from one corner to the other, she forgot all about the innocent girl and got caught up in the game.

The little girl fell.

She hit her head. She was bleeding and crying. Her screams tore my heart. Her white dress was torn and smudged. Her face was covered in dirt.

Her smile sank into her pain.

She dragged her feet to the bathroom ... blood was all over her clothes ... She put the crying baby in the wash basin under running water ... her screams grew louder ... In an attempt to silence her, she put her hand over her mouth ... she pushed harder ... she held her tight ... the girl stopped screaming ... she was no longer crying ... she was not even breathing.

The innocent girl is dead.

It was a mistake. She could not go back to her parents ... she ran away ... she kept running ... the nightmare goes on ...

***

She is a 10-year-old bag of crumbled fat.

At night, when no one could see her bulging tummy and protruding teeth, she would lurk in the dark, staring at the blocks across the street; a tall building, a little villa, and another tall building. Everything looked better at night!

Who is that in the window? A young servant girl studying to change her destiny? A heartbroken teenager whose anguish came between him and sleep? A woman praying? A couple fighting? A murder? There was a story behind each window and a secret life she created for the heroes of her stories.

She has a secret identity too ... a name that means nothing to anyone ... a character with no inhibitions ... a girl who will not be judged ... another chance at life ... the life she could have never lived.

How hard is it to be free? Call me Jenny – Jennifer Anderson.

***

I wrote you many letters in my mind, and in my unsent letters I wanted to tell you that I was hurting; that I made a mistake; that I let you down. At other times I wanted to share with you my conquests; to ask for advice; to beg you to be proud of your very different little girl. But I chose to leave you wondering what was going on in that weird head of mine and I enjoyed that perplexed look on your face. Now I have decided to come forward, summon my courage, and write you a well-earned, well-deserved letter. I will not send it to you in private; I will publish it for the whole world to read.

You have been the subject of my anger, rebellion, and twisted mind for many years. Let me start now by saying "I am sorry ... I am very sorry". Growing up, I thought you did not love me; I craved for warmth and tenderness. I never looked beyond the cool, well-composed façade; I successfully alienated myself from you. Then I began judging you: cold, temperamental, distant, stubborn, materialistic, undiplomatic, isolated, and harsh. My masterpiece was choosing to move out on Mother's Day!

Now that I have a life and a house of my own, I have begun seeing things differently. The first mega revelation is: I am you! Now I understand the kind of responsibilities that can derail a woman from her nature; how the icon of femininity can collapse under the pressures that most men cannot endure; how a hard outer shell is needed to protect a mellow mushy core; how betrayal hurts; how unmet expectations ache; how a heart bleeds when stabbed by a loved one; how a cold shoulder replaces the warm nook when love, respect, and honesty are replaced by lies, abuse, and lethargy. I have had to deal with all the situations that fate handed you and, to my surprise, I was you ... I still am you ... just like you in every aspect.

A few months ago, a friend of mine lost her mother and I went to comfort her. She wanted one last chance to apologize; one last chance to say "I love you". She wanted to bring back every fight and erase it; needed to take back all the bad things she had said or done; wished she had spent more time with her. She already missed her voice when only yesterday she did not want to talk to her. She wanted to hold on to every memory, every scent, and every piece of crappy cloth ... that is all she had left of her mother.

I could only think of you my dear mother. I saw your face, your lovely smile, your kind eyes, and the warmth that I never recognized as a kid, as a teenager, or as the rebellious young woman that I am. Oh my lovely mother, I wronged you so much and you forgave it all; challenged you many times and you helped me win every time; said that you were never there for me, but looking at things now, you were always there one way or the other; accused you of being cold and distant when it was me who never tried to reach out to you; out of my own stubbornness, I insisted that you were stubborn; criticized your choice to be lonely, and then I learned the difference between being lonely and alone; questioned your tact and diplomacy, and who am I to talk? The machine gun without a safety valve?

I have been trapped between the blades of regret and anger. We would have a bad chat and I would dart my angry looks and words at you. The tigress that you wounded with your disapproval lashes back at you with her teeth and claws, trying to defend her individuality and existence; she is fighting the sharp pain of being unaccepted. Then I take my sore wounds home and wallow in regret and guilt. As I attempt to pick up the phone and apologize, I feel the pangs of rejection, and I give in to my worst self. Days pass, you forgive, I pretend to forget, we have another encounter, and then anger strikes, followed by regret, then anger, then regret ... I am so consumed!

Dear mother, it hurts me when I feel that you do not like who I have become. I am what you made me, so please forget about people and society; we owe them nothing. Do not compare me to the image of the girl you would have preferred me to be; look at who I really am. When I moved out I gave my back to a very unhappy time in my life; now I am happy and I want you to be happy too. I want us to be the best friends we never were and I want you to know that I finally understand.

Love ... always and forever,

Me

***

I fell asleep.

I woke up gasping for air. I was late. I missed you. You were gone. Your clothes were gone. Your suitcase was gone. You were on the plane. I went back to sleep feeling a rock on my chest and wetness on my face. Breathing never felt so difficult. I woke up with my fists clenched. I dreamt of you. I no longer dream of you. I was lost. I experienced loss. I am haunted.

You came back nine months later. I have forgotten you. I could only remember my fear when you were gone, my tears when I missed you, my need to throw my little hand in yours, my longing to hear your voice, and the wind blowing through our roof. Why did you have to take the roof?

You left again ... I did not cry.

You came back. Your face has changed. Your eyes wandered in an empty room. Your arms did not hold me as tight. My hands are bigger and stronger. You said you were leaving. You left – again!

I have learned how to be a big girl. I am no longer your little girl. I fell and my dress got dirty. I got up and licked my wounds. I learned how to hide the scars underneath layers of makeup and a smile. You come and go. I am insulated. You are isolated. I no longer cry.

Why did you preach what you never practiced? Why do I confuse protection with possessiveness? Why did you over shelter me? Why did you take the roof away? – It is just so cold and scary.

I am still scared.

Yes ... fear ... you have equipped me with nothing but fear to face the world; fear of the unknown, fear of the obvious, fear of testosterone, fear of estrogen, fear of change, and fear of dreaming. I also fear the day you fail to return. I fear the days you spend away. I fear resenting you for I could only love you. Where did the roof go?

Your daughter,
Me

***

"...maybe that whole love thing is just a grown-up version of Santa Claus; just a myth we've been fed since childhood. So, we keep buying magazines, joining clubs, and doing therapy and watching movies with hit pop songs played over love montages all in a pathetic attempt to explain why our love Santa keeps getting caught in the chimney." - *Meg Ryan as Kate McKay in the movie Kate and Leopold.*

Dear Santa,

I know you are very busy but I really need you to consider my wish. I have been a good girl this last year and I know what I want for a gift this year. I am writing to you a whole month in advance so you can search thoroughly, and I will give you all the clues to help you out of that chimney that you keep getting caught in one year after another. I do not think that you are a myth and I do not think that love is a myth so, my dear love Santa, please read my letter and make my wish come true. I will not ask for more wealth or for better health, nor do I want earthly pleasures or heavenly measures ... I want a man.

I want you to dash through the snow on your sleigh, jingle your bells, and get your elves to run up and down the globe to get me my long-awaited present and, when you get him, skip the chimney part and just leave him on my doorstep. I have always been accused of not knowing what I wanted and of not being decisive, so I will go into the nitty-gritty details because I do not want you to send me the wrong man ... Again! I hope you do not think of me as being bossy; I am just helping you with your hunt, and mine, for Mr. Right.

To help you with the screening process, I will first rule out what I know for sure that I do not want. Married, lost, depressed, expired, or clumsy is out of the question. Narrow-minded, cold-hearted, mind-numbing, or thick-skinned is not even an option. Bad English, bad breath, or bad grooming is a bad gift. Jobless, faithless, or moneyless makes less of a Christmas gift. I do not like quiet, boring, or dull men and I prefer them tall, dark and handsome, but fair, cute and blonde is not crossed out, and he has to like my curls!

Now that I have helped you out with the outline, let's go to a more sophisticated level, and Santa, I have to give you fair warning: this is the level that confuses you the most every year. Make sure this time he is intellectual yet sensitive; sensitive yet masculine; masculine yet tender; tender yet protective; protective but not possessive. Have I said enough? Oh and Santa, my heart has had enough bumps, dumps, and jumps. I have run out of glue mending broken pieces and I have no more tolerance for any more make-ups and break-ups.

Santa, I am not dictating anything; I am just helping you get me the right gift. People say that I am too picky, demanding, and uncompromising, but I am just a girl who wants to take exactly what she is willing to give; I just want to love and to be loved – but I will never love a man unless he has a consensus from my mind, body, and heart. Now that I have gone this far without any divine intervention to stop me from continuing my letter, I will assume that this is a clear sign that you will take my wish seriously this year.

Ah ... one last thing before I seal it with a kiss; no Virgos or Scorpios allowed; I will not even bother you with the reasons! If you find me a Cancerian, send him with a life-time stock of antidepressants, and needless to say that Sagittarian men are known to be so-so in the sack so I will need a money-back guarantee. A refined Leo or a not-so-loud Aries is like looking for a needle in a haystack so forget it. Aquarian guys are sloppy and Geminis are not very straightforward. Pisces are so out of touch with reality, Taurean men love playing grand inquisitor with me, and I do not like either sign. I might consider a Capricorn who puts me next to his career, instead of miles and miles below it. I am a Libra and I am not sure two of me will be a good gift. Don't let that stop you Santa ... work with their ascendants, check their karma, and email me potential resumes so I can pick my gift.

Love,

Me

***

I knew this feeling ... the feeling deep down that the person on the other end of the relationship is slipping away. I knew it was over and I knew that the more I held on, the faster he would slip away ... and the worse I would get hurt!

Getting over someone is hard ... ending a relationship is hard ... overcoming a crush is hard ... letting go is hard ... I wished it would just hurt a bit then go away ... I wished it were as simple as that ...

The hard part is over and I am now vomiting the toxic residues of a relationship that went sour ... the leftovers of a guy who poisoned my life!

At first I felt like I'd been hit by a bus ... I did not want to get out of bed ... I just sat there and hurt from inside ... I could not reach into myself- where it hurt - to try to make it better ... there were tears to go with the pain, and sometimes I just went numb and was then struck by this sudden pain which made me drive like a maniac, shout for no good reason, and feel overwhelmed by anger at him, me, and life.

I tried resisting, but the more I resisted the more difficult it got. It was like pushing a rewind button that would start the cycle all over again.

Then the next natural urge was avoiding my friends ... avoiding the people who would ask me, judge me, blame me, or remind me of the recurrent pattern of choosing the wrong guys. I also avoided those who would pity me, sympathize with me, or make me feel weaker than I already am.

I tried to go out with strangers ... just faces and voices to fill in the empty hole inside me ... but the more I did that the lonelier I felt ... I was always out of place ... I did not belong with them or with anyone else.

I also fell for the common mistake; I tried dating someone else ... it either went totally wrong from the beginning as I tried to prove to myself, subconsciously, that I had lost the only person who was fit to be the perfect match, or it was fun for a few days for novelty's sake, then I lost interest all of a sudden ... I was not motivated to talk to, listen to, or go out with the 'cushion' - yes, that person's function was limited to absorbing the pain of me falling from cloud nine!

Memories hurt ... unfulfilled wishes and dreams hurt ... anger hurt ... the wounded ego of a girl who believed she should have been worshipped hurt...
The hole got deeper ... the wound felt as if it would never heal ... it was a vicious cycle that just drained me.

During that time I had urges to pick up the phone and call ... to send an SMS ... to see if all was well ... to see if I was missed ... to see if my presence ever made a difference. Deep down I wanted to give him another chance to say sorry, but it was always another slap on the face!

The peak periods were driving to, or back from, work, upon waking up, before going to bed, during meals, in the movies, in front of the TV regardless of what I was watching, before a date, on a date, after a date, with family, with old friends, with new friends, at work ... I do not recall the rest of the times when I wanted to shoot myself!

The amazing part was that once I'd hit rock bottom ... there was nowhere to go but up... so bit by bit the pain loosened its firm grip on me ... the crab that squeezed my heart with its clutches let go of what was left of it ... the memories faded away ... the vivid colors, sounds, and scents seemed to have happened a long time ago ... the isolation decreased ... the loneliness became a friend ... I enjoyed my own company again ... the ground felt closer to my feet than to my head and I began to regain balance and interest in my old life and old friends.

***

As I drove to the office on a grey winter's morning, My Immortal was playing on the radio and for a few minutes I was lost in my thoughts; I wondered what Evanescence meant. I took a mental note and decided to check it out when I got to work. The song went on and on; the lyrics and the soul-penetrating voice of Amy Lee touched a place deep down in my heart, reminding me that there is just too much that time cannot erase. Memories raced with my thoughts until I reached my destination, and in my office, I sat myself on my desk, switched on my computer, and looked up the meaning of the word that I had toyed with throughout my drive.

Merriam-Webster's online dictionary said Evanescence means 'to vanish; to dissipate like vapor; to cease to be visible; to disappear'. In a game of word association, using any of those words, would remind the player of mercury, perfume, or any other substance known for vaporizing. Thinking of it myself, the first thought that came to my mind was a visual image of a man who came to our house a few years ago asking for my hand in an arranged marriage setup. My mother was so excited about me meeting Mr. Perfect; he was young, tall, dark, handsome, successful, well-off, and open-minded. Mr. Perfect was willing to see me even though he knew that I was living on my own, I had a career, I travelled a lot, and I was not the compromising type. Mom was certain that she would get to see me in a wedding gown in no time!

As I walked into the room, my eyes captured his deep black eyes, wide smile, and graceful posture. I smiled back at him approvingly, and as the evening went on I realized that he was also charismatic, witty, and had a great sense of humor. My mother was happy with the way the conversation was going and his mother was ever so cheerful.

Suddenly the room was filled with a heavy silence and all heads turned to me as I asked Mr. Perfect if he was the faithful type. The question just flew out of my mouth and it was too late to take it back. In an attempt to pursue the topic I had raised, I said, with a struggling smile, "I mean, will you be able to write me a paper that states that if I catch you cheating on me, you will pay me a million dollars? I would write you the same paper guaranteeing you my faithfulness." Clearly my attempt to sugarcoat my bomb of a question failed as the silence grew louder.

All it took from Mr. Not-So-Perfect was a clear audible "NO" as an answer to my question, to bring my green-eyed monster out of its cave. My mother, totally baffled, asked the guests if they wanted some sweets; but nothing would stop the provoked monster from its righteous attack; I repeated my question again, highlighting the fact that I expected my husband to be loyal; that I liked to play fair and square; that it was a two-way street; that from a religious stance, marital infidelity is a big sin that men and women get stoned to death for.

Again I kept getting nonsensical replies from the groom-to-be. Matrimonial devotion did not seem to suit his notions. After a long debate that brought my mom to the verge of a heart attack, and brought his mother to a noticeable level of disapproval of the bride-to-be, I told him, in one of my super-aggressive tones, "So now you are in our house, looking at my mother, asking to marry me, and you are letting us both know in advance that you would not be faithful?" I was not being sarcastic; this IS what I had heard: "Marry me and I promise to cheat on you." He said nothing, but his body subconsciously turned to face the door, and his mother saved him when she signalled that it was time to leave.

My mother was more than unhappy when they left; she was livid, and she kept wondering what she had done wrong to deserve a daughter like me. I tried to point out to her where I was coming from, but her main argument was that all men were the same and that I was not going to change the world; as long as the husband came back to his house, wife, and kids then he was a good man and a woman should not ask questions that would lead to a confrontation of any kind. This was how a good wife kept the father of her kids and saved her home! She told me over and over that all men have 'little' affairs and women ignore them. She told me that men have different needs and it was their right to attend to those needs. Finally she gave up and gave me that look that signified the end of the discussion, and I left the house.

So for me, in a word association game, evanescence would be associated with marriage vows that evaporate faster than mercury and sink quicker than a lead ball; with love that flees the merciless scars of infidelity; with a melting sense of commitment; with a fading respect for family. This was not the end of the sad story; it got worse when I shared the details of my 'date' with my friends … they called me a fool; told me that there were no more men who wanted to get married; that who cared what a man did outside the house; that what I did not know about would not hurt me. They sounded so much like my mom and I felt alienated from their world.

Of course Mr. Not-So-Perfect had every right to walk away. With his God-given qualities and mouthwatering attributes he could easily land any girl he wanted for a marriage bargain. Why would he bother with me and with my 'radical' opinions? Why did he have to justify his actions and keep his promises? He did not need to resist temptation if he knew in advance that he would be forgiven. Men created a big myth ages ago and women believed it; they claimed that their physical needs are much higher than those of a woman and used that as an excuse to justify their shameful behavior. They said they got bored of 'eating the same dish every day' and they needed the change. They kept feeding women lies for one generation after another. My grandmother, my mother, and my friends fell for that lie and now I am being asked to go with the flow.

I am no longer angry at Mr. Not-So-Perfect … my anger is directed at the girls who suffer from an extreme condition of low self-esteem; who lock their pride in sealed bottles and throw them into oblivion; who willingly subject themselves to the double edge of treason and rejection; who would prefer sleeping with the enemy than sleeping alone. I get bored too; I crave for a change just as much as men do. I needed to feel desirable and wanted when I was 18 and 28 and will when I am 38, 48, 58, and forever. Still, I would respect my vows of loyalty and commitment to my husband. Infidelity hits the woman's pride; takes its toll on her self-esteem; makes her feel rejected, unwanted, and unfit. If only men knew how much damage they were causing and how deep of a scar they were leaving.

Here goes my girlish dream of happily ever after ... to cherish and to hold vanished into thin air ... to love and to honor evanesced into dark vapors ... until death do us part is just an anagram of 'another stupid adult'. Seriously ... reshuffle the letters and you get ANOTHER STUPID ADULT.

***

Once upon a time there was a caveman…

In his bestseller, Men are from Mars, Women are from Venus, Dr. John Gray tackles how men and women handle a problem; men solve their problems by going into their 'cave' and women solve their problems by talking. Dr. Gray made it crystal clear that a woman should not follow her man into his 'cave'; the more she disapproves of the time her man is in the 'cave', the more reluctant he will be to come out! When I first read that book, every thought came as a revelation and I knew exactly how Sir Isaac Newton must have felt when he understood gravity.

I will resist the urge to write about how men see us – women – as the reincarnation of the Macbeth witches when we are blue with sadness or red with anger; how we are expected to be ever-so-cheerful, problem-free, and crisis-proof; how we are supposed to give the benefit of the doubt, put our best foot forward, be flexible, open-minded, and tolerant. Otherwise, I will be just another 'Egyptian girl', which in this context is synonymous with party-pooper, killjoy, flat beer, and wet blanket on a cold winter's night.

In my younger years, I used to take the 'DO NOT DISTURB' sign quite well, but over time that went hand in hand with heartache, and I developed an allergy to caves, cavemen, and 'do not disturb' signs. Experience taught me that men abuse Dr. Gray's 'cave' theory; they use it as an excuse every time they want to end an existing relationship, start a new relationship, or have overlapping relationships. A man in need of space means a man in need of a new hunt; a man on his way to the cave equals a man on his way out of the relationship; a man who wants to think is a man who wants to weigh the 'new cow' versus the 'old cow'.

I packed my suit of armor, nails, claws, hooks, and daggers, took a lifetime supply of chocolate, and my favorite relationship survival tactics books, and I hopped on his boat. Prince Charming entertained me with stories, jokes, and deep conversations that I never thought men were capable of. He opened up to me and communicated with frankness and transparency. Every now and then I would look at my stack of self-defense mechanisms and laugh … "I really will not need any of my weapons this time … lucky me! I finally found 'the different man'!" I thought.
One happy morning I found the famous 'do not disturb' sign sealing his mind, heart, and tongue. He wanted his space and asked for some time to think! The symptoms of my chronic allergy showed on my face, on my body, on my words, on my SMSs, and on my emails … I geared up for war! After exchanging a few angry looks and a handful of accusations, my newly found man went into his cave and I waited outside, praying for the best yet expecting the worst.

Dr. Gray asks women to do something fun and enjoyable while the man is brooding in his cave. So, while my caveman was doing what he needed to do, I fantasized about having a shaved head, adopting a new cat, selling my dining table, going to a tanning salon, starting a match-making service, and other crazy things that would be censored! I avoided any thoughts that would lead me to ask, "What is he doing in his cave?" I did not want to think, did not care to ask, and was not prepared to know.

My caveman was not as bad as the other cavemen out there; we were not totally disconnected ... there was network coverage in the cave and, to me, the phone represented the whole relationship. I got used to the new form of communication, adjusted my expectations of him, kept him archived in that grey zone between a friend and a special friend, and took extra doses of chocolate to alleviate the symptoms of my allergy to cavemen. Finally he poked his head out of his cave, told me that he hated women, and then went back into hibernation. I stood there wondering if I was cursed or if a wicked fairy had put a spell on me when I was born to get back at my parents!

The caveman handed me a piece of paper that symbolized his new calling in life: he was going lead a 'men's liberation movement'. He would spend what was left of his life advocating male rights in a female-governed community. He would free men from their oppressors ... women! The wicked witches – us – would be tied to a stake and burned to death. Egyptian women today have well-paying jobs, leading positions, have no time for being mothers, know nothing about being wives, and are materialistic, demanding, and manipulative. They are compulsive liars, ugly double-faced creatures, and they nag, nag again, and nag more.

The list of demands was not long, but it was extremely creative and original. The caveman wanted to switch places with women; he would stay home and take care of the kids while she had to work, make money, get him a maid, pay the bills, take him to nice places, spend regular vacations, and get him anything he pointed a finger at. On behalf of men, he was pleading for equality; a man usually got his bride an engagement ring or shabka, so why doesn't she get him something, within the same price range, as well? He is asked to pay money in advance before the marriage like a dowry or mahr and he writes another sum that he has to pay if he divorces her. My ingenious caveman wanted men to stop paying the mahr, or else women had to pay an equal amount. He also wanted the 'in-case-of-divorce' money to be a debt on whoever asked for a divorce.

The caveman was urging men to give women what they have always asked for – their liberation; hence, no man should pick up a check, open a door, or carry a heavy bag on behalf of a woman. There were some miscellaneous items on the list: Egyptian women were fake, full of pretence, and had petty minds and little brains. Once their biological clock started ticking, they would go on a relentless man-chase trying to get a package that looked and felt good, paid and lived well, and wanted to settle down. They want a big wedding to show off, a honeymoon to get their friends envious, and a man pour la forme ... women in this country look better and are more socially accepted when they are dangling from a man's arm!

At first I was angry, and the feminist in me wanted to smash his head - and his cave. Then I felt a lot of sympathy gushing through my heart; many Janes had stepped over the heart of my poor Tarzan. Then I decided to write back a plea in defense of women and condemning men, as I always do. I started with the history of the women's liberation movement and what evoked it – namely men abusing women on the grounds of having to provide for them. In plain English: I shelter you, feed you, clothe you, protect you, and get you pregnant before it is too late for you to have kids, then I am a man and you, as a woman, should be silently grateful to have me in your life, even if I beat you up, don't give you enough money, have affairs, get a second wife, or just act like a complete jerk.

But when I came to the actual demands - his demands that reflect how women act nowadays and how Egyptian society has become a foster home for the seven deadly sins including greed, gluttony, lust, and sloth -, I had nothing to say in our defense. He was right! We have made men view us as bloodthirsty hounds aiming at their lives! Then I realized why Egyptian men prefer dating or marrying foreign ladies. Those blondes do not just have the looks; they have what it takes to bring out the best in our men. They believe in them and in their innate qualities; unlike us, they give them names, not labels; they want to share and give; they want to build a life based on honesty, trust, and respect, while we tend to put the cash, the car, the wedding, the villa, the honeymoon, the ring, and all the other stuff on the one hand, and on the other sits the caveman ... alone ... thinking of going back into his cave for shelter.

***

I did not lose sight of the cave for a few weeks. I got a comfortable chair and seated myself at the door, waiting for any sign of life from my caveman. When the sitting, the thinking, and the waiting took their toll on my body, mind, and soul, I would hover around the cave, partly to make sure that the caveman was still breathing and partly to make sure that there was no one else breathing inside with him ... yes, I had my doubts!

Finally, I took pity on my poor soul and decided to end my misery. With a strong dose of determination, I got on my feet, pushed the chair away, looked at the cave one last time, then turned my back and left. I let go! I left my safe and secure spot in front of his cave and walked back into the jungle. I grew a beard and a moustache, put on a suit, got a gun, gave my brain a break, replaced my heart with a rock, and made my grand entrance into the jungle as a man. I became everyman's best buddy. I had a mission; I wanted to know how such creatures think, the way they perceive women, and their decoding of our messages.

My first tour in Tarzan's world focused on his relationship with Jane. When I was in Jane's shoes I was baffled by the sudden deterioration in the curve of the relationship. Why would Tarzan start with so much interest and persistence, then he would contract a sudden relationship atrophy syndrome and turn his coldest shoulder to the same Jane he had once pursued with so much adamancy?

Now, being an implanted bug in Tarzan's little head, I saw with his eyes, spoke with his tongue, and felt with his senses. Every Tarzan was born a hunter. He hunts for shelter, food, and love. Tarzan would never live in a ready-made house, eat prey that dropped dead at his feet, or get serious with a Jane who is a genie at his command. I saw Janes drooling at the sight of a Tarzan; they seemed to come back to life from the land of the dead once they laid eyes on a potential Tarzan. They shamefully fell for his oldest manoeuvres, turned their backs on common sense, willingly blinded themselves to his real intentions, and got on a temporary high just to have the blessing of a Tarzan for a few days!

Being a Tarzan in disguise, men handed me their well-kept secrets and told me bluntly how a Jane can lose a Tarzan in ten days by making ten fatal mistakes. I took mental notes, wrote in shorthand, and recorded what I could on tape. I knew I had to share this revelation with my fellow Janes.

First mistake: Delete "yes" from your vocabulary. Tarzans get motivated the more they hear you say "no". Let's meet after work, NO! Let's have breakfast, lunch or brunch, or supper or dinner, NO! Let's watch a movie – at home or in the movie theater – NO! Let's spend a few nights in Agami, Sharm, or anywhere on planet Earth, NO! Let's meet every day, NO! Let's hang out every night, NO! But remember, too little is just as bad as too much.

Second mistake: For some reason, women tend to think that Tarzans are naïve – FICTION! Men have a lie detector built into their software. Lie a white lie and he will question your breathing. Lie a colored lie and you lost his trust forever.

Third mistake: Never dump a current Tarzan for a new Tarzan thinking that the newcomer will be flattered. Men share a golden rule that says that if a woman dumps a man for him, she is most likely to dump him for another man. You are just giving him a valid reason to take you for a ride ... a quick one!

Fourth mistake: Resist physical intimacy! Men do not understand any of your reasons; feeling close and cozy, attachment and self expression, love at first sight, genuine care, and any other reason you might have are not decodable by Tarzans. All your messages in this area will be translated into one word and its derogative synonyms ... EASY! (This rule applies for the first ten hours, days, weeks, and months – if possible!)

Fifth mistake: Enthusiasm ... big blunder girls! Curb your enthusiasm. Lock up the thrill in your voice, the spark in your eyes, the pounding of your heart, and the wide smile that brightens your face when you meet or talk to your Tarzan. Let him work for it ... they truly like to work hard.

Sixth mistake: Generation after generation, men have become immune to our natural charms and allergic to pretence. Ladies, you need to strike a balance between coming across as arrogant, fake, and conceited on the one hand, and being meek, genuine, and clumsy on the other.

Seventh mistake: Don't nag or plague, hunt or haunt, or stalk or chase your new Tarzan. Give him space to miss you, time to show it, and a chance to express it. Men hate leeches and any type of insect with hanging-on characteristics. They also dislike whining.

Eighth mistake: Men are not very fond of shadows; shadows can give them a heart attack or an urge to run. Calling him first thing in the morning, on the way to work, when you reach work, at mid-day, mid noon, and midnight is bad. Showing up at his door step anytime and all the time is not good either. Avoid the classic mistake of being a 'thing' in his car, a 'thing' in his house, or a 'thing' in his life.

Ninth mistake: He is not my boyfriend yet – read it, write it, and use it every time you feel jealous, possessive, or inquisitive. He is still a free man, and so are you. He owes you nothing, and neither do you.

Tenth mistake: Madonna's Material Girl is out of fashion. Tarzans do not like Janes who love their car, villa, and bank account. They abhor being treated as packages of assorted goodies, so if you fail to like a man for who he is, not for what he stands for, then walk away while you still can. Tarzan will spare no effort to humiliate you as a punishment for such a grave offence against his mighty self.

***

Clap Clap, girls and boys are playing musical chairs ... an easy game on the dating scene ... just jump on an empty chair ... just get an available guy ... just get an available girl ... and as you let go of her, make sure you grab another girl ... as you jump boats, make sure you left nothing behind ... ditch your partners ... switch your partners ... just keep going in circles around the musical chairs ...

What is happening to us? How did we get trapped in an endless game of musical chairs? Why did we agree to the rules of play? Who told us not to stop? Guys, why do you play ball with your girls? Girls, why do you play dummies with your guys? Isn't it sad? Isn't it pathetic? Isn't it disgusting?!! False pretences, facades, manoeuvres, fake words, shallow appearances, and out-of-this-world expectations rule this fiasco.

Egyptian men are caught between what they like and what they want; they like the girls that their minds do not want and they want the girls that their hearts do not like. A typical example of this schizophrenic condition is the single version of the cool guy who is seen in all the trendy hangouts. He drinks, dances, flirts, dates, and the sky is the limit when it comes to how far he could go with his adventures. Mr. Cool likes girls who share his wild rides and challenge his hunter instinct; who are exposed, experienced, and expressive.

If it is just dating and having a nice time, Mr. Cool has no problem. But when it comes to the forever word, Mr. Cool takes off his cool mask and in a strict tone describes the girl he wants: traditional, conservative, religious, sheltered, and controllable. But is Mr. Cool willing to alter his lifestyle? Is he willing to become an equal match for the girl he wants? No! No! This is not how this story goes. Mr. Cool will eventually get married to a girl who will not threaten his sense of security; who has no benchmarks against which to measure his performance, in and out of bed; who is just grateful to have him in her life. Then he will leave her at home to take care of his house and his kids while he pursues the girls he *likes*.

This is not the end of Mr. Cool ... you will see the married version of Mr. Cool in the colleague who hits on you at work, in the client who puts you in one hand and the business deal in the other, in the werewolf who hunts you during outings and chases you at parties – all of them sounding like a broken record when they tell you how unhappy they are in their marriages; how they need someone who understands them and shares their dreams; how they miss communication and passion in their homes ... sounds too familiar?!!!

Egyptian girls, on the other hand, have lost touch with who they really are and what they really want. Most of us do not know what we like any more. As 'good girls' we should dress in a certain way, go out to specific places, be seen in the company of particular people, be home by this or that socially agreed upon time, and the 'good girl' list goes on. It is as if we were born into this world to meet other peoples' expectations, regardless of who we are. Our dreams are always blurred by the influence of a higher authority that dictates the code of conduct we should abide by to gain acceptance.

Someone once told me that human beings have three dimensions: how you see yourself, how others see you, and how you want others to see you. The closer the distance between the three dimensions, the more at peace you are and the more stable you become. How many girls do you see stretching their three dimensions east, west, south, and north every day? They are bending over backwards, denying their needs, turning against their true selves. Take a close look at a sequence of actions that contradict the words, words that defy the body language, and body language that is at war with the eyes - all in an attempt to meet expectations, gain respect, get approval, and win a ring on the naked left finger!

If girls compare their expectations of a man when they were sixteen and what they are willing to accept from a man now, they will see how far they are willing to compromise. Is it growing up or growing desperate that drives us so far down the ladder of expectations? An assembled package of your average guy replaced the tailor-made Prince Charming; a married man will do if he has the money, a younger guy will do if he has the looks, any man will do if he can make it to the alter!

The cycle continues and, like a game of cards, when you throw a card away someone picks it up, and when you pick up a new card you have to know that it was thrown away by another player in the game. With a mask on his face he promises to love her forever, and with a mask on her face she swears

she has never played before. The music is still playing ... cards are handed ... cards are thrown ... chairs are vacant ... chairs are taken ... and the game goes on!

Bang Bang, you shot me down, Bang Bang, I hit the ground, Bang Bang, that awful sound, Bang Bang, my baby shot me down!

***

Before I start my story with Mr. Big, I would like to draw a simple, yet clear, profile of such a mind-blowing character ... Mr. Big ... I am sure you've come across a Mr. Big at least once in your life.

He walks in a room with his head stuck up; his big smile covers layers of confidence alternating with other layers of high self-esteem. He is known for daring eye contact and can mesmerize you with a naughty gaze before you even mention your name to him. He has the air of a Jane Austen aristocratic hero and his words, jokes, and stories will make your hand-watch obsolete.
Hold your horses, girl! Mr. Big's big ego is big enough to swallow you, your pride, and your dreams of a happily-ever-after ending with this charmer. Your slow walking, slow talking hero will walk you to the verge of insanity and will talk you into changing your car, your look, your house, your friends, and he might go as far as your mother, father, brothers, and sisters. He is ready to whip you with sarcasm and nothing, absolutely nothing, will stop him but a knife in his heart or a plate in his face.

Mr. Big will smash your big toe under his big foot and your big love will be expelled in seconds out of his big heart. He will wear his big black suit, put on his big black sunglasses, get in his big black car, and will leave you to suffer alone in a big black hole after he has made his big black exit.

Back to me and my story with Mr. Big; we met ... chemistry was there ... interest was there, and it was time to get a bit up-close and personal ... I got out of bed, brushed off my laziness, and jump-started my mind to prepare myself for the first real date with Mr. Big.

We met, we sat, we ate, we talked, we laughed, and then we got really comfortable with the conversation.

Me: Now that I have talked enough about me and my stories, tell me about the girls you have sent home with a flea in their ear.

Mr. Big: *(Trying to adopt a humble tone)* Oh they are so many ... I have dated half of the girls in Egypt and they are just not what I am looking for. You see I am not looking for a perfect girl; I am just looking for the perfect match.

Me: *(Trying not to look worried about my future)* What went wrong?

Mr. Big: Well, there was this girl who was perfectly attuned to me; she knew when to call, when to back off, when to listen, when to talk, BUT she had a temper issue; she could not control her temper when I lost mine.

To myself: You are lucky I am in a good mood today or I would have introduced YOU to MY temper problem. Then I managed to conjure a smile and, in a peaceful tone, I asked Mr. Big to continue.

Mr. Big: There was another girl who was such a party pooper. She was smart, career-oriented, understood me, but she always managed to spoil our happy moments. She was so jealous of any girl I talked to. I know I flirt and she knows I flirt, but I am with her ... why does she let jealousy take over?

(He really looked oblivious to the reasons of her jealousy; I almost sympathized with him!)

Me: Oh it must be her insecurities taking over. Okay, enough about those poor unfortunate girls; tell me about the girls who said no.

Mr. Big: I do not understand.

Me: *(Trying to talk slower than usual)* You know, we all have had our share of rejection ... So maybe you liked a girl and she was not interested, or maybe you went out a few times then she lost interest ... you know, the same old story.

(Now the smile was struggling on my face.)

Mr. Big: None

Me: None what?

Mr. Big: No girl has ever said no to me. I have never been turned down by a girl. No girl who knew me has lost interest; as long as I am interested I will keep her interested; if I lose interest she might have a chance to lose interest too, but usually she is too hooked up to break free.

(I was really suffering.)

Me: Tell me then what makes you think that no girl will say no to you ... no I am not interested, or no I lost interest? *(I am going to nail him now.)*

Mr. Big: I am very self-confident. I know who I am, who my family is, I have an impressive career plus I am smart, witty, fun, and handsome. *(Mr. Big explained with a reassuring giggle.)*

Me: *(God, what have I gotten myself into?)* Ok ... I see your point. So Mr. Perfect, what are you looking for in your perfect match?

Mr. Big: *(With the look of a little boy who is looking forward to the next visit to the candy store)* A girl with brains, who knows what she wants out of life, who has a life, who has a career, who has an opinion, who is responsible yet dependent on me, who is feminine but not vulnerable, who knows when to come close and when to give me space, who is fun, loving, and caring, who is decent, respectable, and presentable, who is not clingy, insecure, or sticky, who is herself and is not fake.

(Here I smiled and thought that the guy was not asking for much; then I was summoned back to earth when Mr. Big continued.)

Mr. Big: This is not all of course; this is the core, but there are other things that make the girl win or lose points: there is the family, the upbringing, the education, the hobbies, the interests, her choice of friends, her attitude in public, and her social status.

(Mr. Big turned to me all of a sudden and asked me about what I was looking for in a man.)

***

"I broke up with her … she is not a virgin." With these words, my best friend, Sparky, woke me up on a lovely sunny Friday. I got into my lazy weekend outfit and drove to that sunny promenade downtown to meet him. My mind was still asleep; I was not sure what I had to say to him, and I did not know what to expect to hear about her. Shania Twain's ominous song, It only hurts when I am breathing, was playing on the radio and my heart went out to the poor girl Sparky had broken up with the night before, yet I decided to keep my thoughts to myself and listen to him with an objective pair of ears.

I pulled up a chair, adjusted it to face the sun, ordered a hot cup of tea with mint, looked at Sparky with big green eyes, and told him to tell me what had happened. He moved a nervous hand through his tousled black hair and told me, in the saddest tone ever, "She deceived me … I fell in love with a slut … I will make her pay for it!" My lovely Friday was ruined as I asked him to tell me what had turned his angel into a slut overnight.

"I told you … she is not a virgin … she confessed yesterday … I asked her if she had done it before and I was sure she would say she had not … she looked so innocent … but instead she told me she had … I went deaf, then numb, then mad, and I broke up with her … what more do you want to know?" Sparky barked back at me.

"Take it easy now and let's break this down into little pieces," I said carefully, trying not to infuriate him. As I avoided the slightest eye contact, I took a sip of my tea and asked him, "Ok … she is not a virgin … what does this say about her?"

Sparky did not take much time to think. "She is a slut; she is loose; she is easy; she cannot be trusted; she is not fit to be either a wife or a mother; she did it before marriage and she is most likely going to do it after marriage." He said this with utter confidence; and as though his problem was suddenly resolved with this conclusion, he asked for the check, thanked me for my support, and left.

My drive home was far from pleasant; I was angry! My sense of justice had been provoked and I could see visions of me whipping all the Sparkys in the world with my counter argument. I wanted to pick up the phone and tell my best friend that he was a big fat fake lie; that he was a selfish egocentric sexist; that I envied his ex-girlfriend for getting rid of him while I was stuck with him in this so-called friendship.

This was not fair! He had called her a slut, denied her the right to be a wife and a mother, turned her into a cheap piece of meat, and decided that she would cheat on whoever decided to take pity on her and marry her. What about the other side of the coin? What about the accomplice in the crime? What about you, Sparky? Are you a virgin? Well, I know you are not! I know you have done it, bragged about it, and never missed a chance to blow your own horn when it came to talking about it. He had turned a human being into a chocolate bar and he wanted to be the first to unwrap the chocolate bar!

Now what does that say about the Sparkys we know? What does that say about our society? For him it is a subject worthy of pride, appreciation, and admiration, while for her it is a subject of shame, humiliation, and disgrace. He brags about his big deeds to every Tom, Dick, and Harry, while she strives to bury the deep dark secret. His mom proudly jokes about his adventures and his dad gives him well-kept advice, while her family, if they found out, would rather she had caught an exotic disease and died when she was a child.

Agreeing that in the eyes of God males and females are judged on the same criteria, let's dig deep into the attitude of Sparky. Let's try to figure out why men, in our male-dominated society, think and behave like that. Let's also find out the reasons that make girls accept that behavior. Why is experience an advantage on his side and a disadvantage on hers? Why does he expect her to forgive and forget about his past while he insists on a detailed confession of her amours? Well, Sparky, I know you are not going to like the answers I came up with.

It can all be traced back and tied down to insecurity. Sparky is, after all, a scared little boy who does not want to be evaluated, judged, or measured up, or down, against benchmarks from her previous relationships. He is a lazy male prototype who does not want to work hard to keep her happy, satisfied, and fulfilled in their marriage. He does not want her to compare notes and give grades. He does not want to hear comments, remarks, or observations from her; he just wants his cute doll to look at him with grateful eyes and thank him for being in her life. He does not want to listen to her needs; he wants to hear how good he makes her feel and how much of an expert he is.

Sparky wants to play master-slave with her; she will never complain, leave him, or get a life, while he is busy with his wild goose chases. She will never threaten to walk out on their marriage, or dump him for negligence and first-degree murder of the love she had for him. He wants to be the source of whatever sexual knowledge she acquires, and as her sole and prime teacher he will teach her the uses and benefits of yes, *thank you, and you are the best!*

Now let's examine her ... what is wrong with us girls? Why do we let the Sparkys get away with it? I know it is easier asked than answered ... but let me try ... it is years and generations of accumulated traditions that have tied our hands to our feet, blindfolded our eyes, and gagged our mouths. I could not tell Sparky to his face that he was a hypocrite; if she was loose then he was loose and if she would cheat on her husband then he would cheat on his wife. For having sex, he could not trust her, so why would any other girl trust him?

She could have easily lied ... she could have easily 'rewrapped' the chocolate bar. The price of a pair of Italian boots would have saved her pride and would have made her a happy bride. When she was honest she was rejected. Sparky did not appreciate the fact that she respected him enough to tell him the truth. I am sure that next time she will get smarter and swear on her mother's life that she does not know how babies are made, and I am sure that the next Sparky, like all the other Sparkys, would rather be lied to than be faced with such an ugly truth! I wonder how happy the next Sparky will be with his brand new rewrapped chocolate bar.

In our circles we see a lot of 'chocolate bars' who hold on to the wrapping, but we all know how they went from one hand to the other. There are girls who literally got naked with so many men yet managed to hold on to that little piece of skin that, in the eyes of Sparky, makes a girl an angel or a slut. Egyptian men are not thinking straight ... a slut is not a label; it is a whole attitude of a girl who is willing to lie, cheat, and twist facts ... a virgin is not a medical term; it is a girl who is honest, pure, and sincere ... a girl is not a chocolate bar, and Sparkys are definitely not Smarties.

I am not promoting premarital sex; I am neither defending girls who lost their virginity nor attacking guys who want to be the first to unwrap the chocolate bar ... I am just asking how can a society applaud something when it is done by one gender and then condemn that very same thing when it is done by the other gender, knowing that all religions forbid that thing? How can a man choose a lie over the truth? How can God's most favored creature be so ruthless and judgmental when it comes to his female counterpart? How do I tell Sparky what I really think of him?

***

She was young, cheerful, and buzzing with life. He was a dream come true: well-educated, well-mannered, good looking, and successful. I went out with them a few times but I did not feel very welcomed; he was civil but cold and we just did not blend as a group. She was blown away by her new amour and did not notice that we did not do anything together anymore. Nonetheless, I was happy for *her*, resided in the back seat, and kept my mouth shut.

We met every once in a while to catch up, and he was all we talked about - which was fine by me until all I heard from *her* was: "I am not feeling well", "I am out of my mood", "I miss my friends", "I am so lonely", "Am I pretty?", "I want to leave him", "I can't leave him", "I left him", "We are back together", "I made him hit me when I insisted on talking about us right after he came from work", "He apologized", "How do I hide that bruise?" ... and more.

He sucked the life out of *me* and let me down a million times; I was emotionally blackmailed into a relationship that seemed to drag on forever. Yesterday, we had a fight and his fingers were printed in blue on *my* cheek. I could hear '*me*' sobbing. I am not sure what hurts more: the bruises on *my* face, the wounds in *my* heart, the deep scar in *my* pride, the poison in *my* veins, or the longing for *my* old self and old life?

He made *me* feel as if he was a gift sent by God to pull *me* out of a stinking brothel! He hated all my friends who envied *me* for having him! He hit *her* when he had a tough day at work! *She* is a bitch if *she* has a social life! *She* is pushing her body onto men if *she* dresses nicely! *She* is not allowed to argue with him in private and is forbidden from voicing a contradicting opinion, or any opinion, in public! I literally had to report to him; I was accountable for every what, when, where, why, who, which, how, and how often that took place today, might take place tomorrow, and that took place last year, the year before, or ten years ago! On the other hand, *she* was not allowed to complain, question, or inquire. *She* cannot say "*no*" or *she* will be express shipped to lonely island again. *She* was robbed of *her* right to choose and denied *her* right to be fulfilled.

I was a 24/7 slave in the dungeons of a cruel, merciless master she called boyfriend! She was starved of love and attention, humiliated in private and public, emotionally blackmailed, brainwashed, forced into sex, cheated upon, restricted, isolated, intimidated, neglected, and beaten up! What was *my* excuse? Ah, yes … it was the fear of loneliness; this was the knife that the loving boyfriend held to *her* throat and stuck in *her* heart. *She* had to obey and conform to the rules or else *she* would be abandoned – *she* would have the 'I am single' stigma for life. No man would take *me*, no one would want me, and I would grow old and die alone!

The trick was to get the 'slave' to depend on her 'master' when it came to social acceptance, some care, infrequent attention, physical gratification, financial support, or any other dangling carrot that would keep her locked up in the cage.

She knew how hard it was to break free from his chains. She worried about his reaction, she was not sure if she could face the world on her own, and she preferred the devil she knew to the many other devils out there that she was too scared to know.

***

I feel empty – 100% empty. There is a huge void in the center of my body; I have no feelings, no passion, no ideas, no thoughts, no drive, and no life. I am a drained air-vacuumed sac of human bones! Last month was very tough. Yes ... again ... I am heartbroken! But this time I am comfortably numb about it. I am just eternally grateful for having a consuming career, great friends, and two adorable cats who always manage to put a smile on my face.

I got an email from a friend who was trying to cheer me up. I opened the email and found a song attached with a note wishing me a quick recovery, and a big hug. I downloaded the song and played it as I flipped though some dusty letters that had been on my desk for a week. My eyes widened and my limp body began showing signs of life again as I heard Shania Twain say, "It's amazing what a little polish'll do: Men are like shoes." I pushed the stop button and then I replayed the song, this time giving it my full attention.

"Men are like shoes, made to confuse ... I don't know which ones to choose ... some you wear in, some you wear out, and some you wanna leave behind ... some make you feel ten feet tall, some make you feel so small ... and some you wanna leave out in the hall or make you feel like kicking the wall ... Some clean up good, just like new... some you can't afford, some are real cheap... Some are good for bumming around on the beach ... I ain't got time for the flip-flop kind... Men are like shoes." The song goes on listing the types of 'shoes' and the analogy between men and shoes just brightened my dreary day.

I needed to hear this; someone, or something, had to remind me of who I am and what I have always stood for. Shania Twain woke me up from my long, tame sleep. I have known him for a year now, and he started as a compromise for me. I settled for the very wrong pair of shoes; uncomfortable from the start, though highly maintained, they lost their allure as time passed, and I realized that I have invested a fortune of emotions into a fake, yet well-polished pair of mismatched sneakers.

The design of this ungodly footwear always set me off balance; I tripped on every stone and landed on my face, on my knees, or on my back many a time. Such shoes should come with a warning: 'For short walks only'. Silly me, I thought I was taking a lovely walk in a green park when I brilliantly exhausted my feet taking long, painful strides on a treadmill that got me nowhere; no matter how long I walked, it only got me as far as an arm's length. All the effort I put in was recorded on the calorie scale but never showed on the distance counter. I kept coming back to frustrating square one!

It is normal to pick up the wrong type of shoes every now and then – all women do that; but only smart women give a wrong pair away. The rest of us hold on to even the ugliest flip-flops out of fear of walking barefoot. We pile up old shoes and unwanted slippers to save face on a day when we have nothing to wear. I preferred to be with a man who made me feel like a big nothing than to being alone. From the start, I accepted his bad moods, destructive phases, sudden disappearances, unjustified aloofness, and patronizing attitude. He took me for granted and I have no one else to blame but myself.

My attitude was a clear 'It's OK to hurt me' sign. I gave him permission to take me for one ride after the other, allowed him to step all over my ego, and blessed his devilish arguments to keep myself trapped in his dungeons. I thought I was stuck in shoes that constantly hurt my toes, while all my friends clearly saw that I was walking barefoot on eggshells. Finally I ended it; with tears rolling down my cheeks, I tossed the annoying shoes out of the car window when I was driving home after my last meeting with him. I painfully sobbed, not knowing what hurt more; my feet, my head, or my heart? I was just hurting all over.

I have not seen him in a couple of months and I have missed him. I have missed his smile; longed to see him moving his fingers through his hair; needed to look into his eyes; yearned to have a physical place in his energy field. Though they were all he wanted, phone calls were not enough for me. We talked daily for many hours on the phone; chatted about common friends, childhood stories, fears, theories, jokes, dreams, and ghosts - yes, right, ghosts! People thought we did not meet because I was always busy; the truth is, he did not care to see me. I turned my eyes away from this fact for a very long time; it was about time I faced the truth!

Still tears replaced the smile the minute my eyes met the cold, stiff look in his eyes. A sharp pain seized me but, like a brave girl, I greeted him with a faint voice and put on a natural, casual look hoping that things would get better. I was with him, yet I never felt more distant; his vibes were cold, his face was expressionless, his eyes were avoiding me, and I did not see one smile cross his face in the two hours that I was with him. I was fighting back tears. I decided to leave; I knew what was coming next and I wanted to be alone when I fell apart. He courteously asked me to stay, but I did not feel a shred of sincerity in his words. I insisted on leaving and he let me go, not knowing that this was the last time he was ever going to see me.

It was always about him and his moods, needs, and phases. At the back of my mind I thought of how it was never about me; how I have been so unfair towards myself. I accepted a lot of baloney hoping that the tight, uncomfortable shoes would loosen up and fit me better; what a dreamer! If the mold is a misfit, the design is ugly, and there is no quality in the finishing, a wrong pair of shoes will be nothing but a pain in the toes! I told him that I would never forgive him for insulting me that way, asked him to never ever call me, ended the conversation, and threw him and everything he stood for out of the window.

And the song goes on: "Tell me about it ... Ooh! Men: have you ever tried to figure them out? Huh, me too, but I ain't got no clue: how about you? ... You've got your kickers an' your ropers, your every-day loafers, an' some that you can never find. You've got slippers an' your zippers, your grabbers and your grippers, an' man, don't you hate that kind? ... Sometimes you hate 'em, an' sometimes you love 'em, I guess it all depends on which way you rub 'em, But a girl can never have too many of 'em."

***

Helen Keller said that the most beautiful things in this world cannot be seen or touched; they must be felt with the heart. My Forrest Gump flew cross the Atlantic leaving Uncle Sam and, like a stray cat, found a nook in my busy life in Cairo. His raw, untamed nature startled me; his strong southern accent, outdated haircut, rough uneven nails, timeless shoes, and colorful shirts repelled part of me, yet attracted another. Wearing D&G as if it were Old Spice, eating rice with a spoon, cutting veal with the fork, walking like a soldier, and cheekily glancing at my curves with the eyes of a curious teenage boy made me realize that he had had a rough ride to wealth and success.

His spelling mistakes, grammar errors, and sentence blunders put a question mark after his education, upbringing, and background. My Forrest Gump missed out on all my witty comments and sarcastic remarks; I had to stick to the basics and I kept it short and simple. He resisted opening up at first, but I comforted him into sharing by talking a bit about myself. I did not want to know the man he is now, with the big company car, company apartment, and expatriate package. I wanted to meet the kid, the teenager, and the young man he left back home many years ago. My 40-year-old Forrest talked about poverty, neediness, and suffering. I saw a strong-willed man driven by admirable ambition; with basic education, minimal reading, primitive brains, and slower-than-usual understanding, Forrest Gump turned everything he touched into gold.

He talked about his achievements with a lot of passion, and I fully understood where that came from. There was a very familiar pitch of pride in his tone and I knew exactly how he felt. I was moved by his untainted nature; I am allergic to fakeness. Were they in his shoes, a lot of Egyptian, or non-Egyptian, men would buy 'social polish' with their money. I have met many men here who learned how to talk smart, dress well, and walk with their heads stuck up high, covering up their modest upbringing. Designer clothes will fit anyone who has the money, and expensive watches will never fall off the thick wrist of a social climber. My Forrest Gump did not buy himself new table manners, grooming habits, or an *en vogue* wardrobe.

Like Forrest Gump, he had lovely blue eyes and an unsuspecting smile; he was muscular and hard in all the right places (no pun intended). I saw a lot of beauty in this simpleton and, being the dreamer that I am, I wanted him to be as wise, as kind, and as innocent as the 1994 Forrest Gump version. I should have known better! Didn't my grandma tell me that looks can be misleading and that outer beauty does not have to mirror inner beauty? Hadn't I fallen into that trap before? I never thought that after three dates, he would star in my book! He triggered fear - a feeling that I locked up deep down in my heart! Something about him scared me.

His vibes were rough and his hands held mine firmly, stopping the flow of air inside my lungs. His eyes were not sincere, his stories were always incomplete, and the numbers did not add up: married at 19, had a daughter at 17, she is now 24, married again at 37, his daughter is 8, got divorced 8 years ago, the girl was 2 years old, and now he is 40! He talked a lot about oil massages and 'doing it', and he did not seem to understand anything I said about time, bonding, mental connection, and emotional spark. In another attempt to curb the horny toad between his legs, I told him that I am stubborn and that 'no' is my natural response to any request. I clearly explained that I liked to hunt and that I was not looking for a one-night stand or a physical adventure.

My version of Forrest Gump had the memory of a fish and the IQ of a sparrow; he could not pronounce my two-syllable Egyptian name, forgot half of the things he told me and all the things I told him, and asked me the same questions at least five times on our three dates. I was faced with two questions more often: first was why I liked him, and second was why I was comfortable with him. Looking back at the whole picture now, my answer should have been, "I have no clue!" I neither liked him nor disliked him; he did not give me tangible reasons for either feeling. All I had to hold onto were his vibes and my gut feeling. As usual, my mind rejected him, my body lusted after him, but my heart feared him. He lost!

My Forrest Gump evoked my instinctive need to run; I felt threatened, and his attitude intimidated the little girl in me. Gump looked at me all of a sudden and said that he was not a freak! My heart skipped a beat! I looked at my drunken partner with wide perplexed eyes as he told me ... again and again ... that I have killer eyes and a killer smile. I just wanted to run. Like Jenny Curran, in the original Forrest Gump, I prayed, "Dear God, make me a bird so I could fly far! Far far away from here!" As I stood there in the street waiting for the valet to bring my car, I struggled to release my hands from his. He wanted to come home with me, or me to go home with him. Again he was pushing and again I was stubborn ... I freed my hand, got in my car, drove off, and did not look behind as Jenny Curran's words echoed louder and louder in my head: Run Forrest! Run! ... Run Jenny! Run!

***

I love sunset tea on the terrace with my mom; I love the tea, the sunset, the mint in the tea, her cat playing with the teabag, but I hate the conversations she strikes up! I was enjoying a great moment watching a lovely bird flying in utter freedom across the horizon when my mom broke into my space capsule and asked me: "Why did your last engagement last three days?" I was too perplexed to reply when she hit me with the second bomb of a question: "Why did you break up with your first fiancé two months before your wedding?" I was still trying to figure out where these darts were coming from when she hit me with: "Why are you still single?" By the time words found their way to my mouth, she was already stoning me with her questions: "What was wrong with H, A, M, K, B, T. R, N, O, S, E, Z ....? Why did you turn down C, D, X, F, G, I, J, L, P, Q, U, V, W, Y ....? Why don't you get married to one of your friends? Why do you have brothers that I never gave birth to? Don't you want to have a baby? Don't you want to have a home? Don't you want to be happy?"

My mind got on the time machine and I remembered the first marriage proposal I got; I was 16 and he was 22. I remember feeling flattered, excited, and important; I was already dreaming of the ring, the wedding, the dress, the honeymoon, and the home. As a little girl my granny, the best story-teller ever, used to tell me nice stories that involved mainly princes, castles, white horses, and happily ever after. It was not difficult for the little girl in me to wear the crown and gown, and ride behind Prince Charming for an eternity of love and happiness. My mother, grandmothers, aunts, and any woman who ever set foot in our house wished me one thing: A man who would take care of me and make me happy!

Judging by the standards of our society, I was a 'normal' girl growing up; I had nothing against men, marriage, kids, and mothers-in-law. When I turned 20, all the heads turned to look at the lucky man whose ring would adorn my finger. Years later, I am still single, and I have gone through a great metamorphosis since my teen years. Countless men have come my way; I have seen those who stink in the mind, those who stink in the heart, and those who stink in the flesh! They all just stink!

That day on her terrace, my mom cross-examined me, questioned my sanity, and was totally oblivious of my motives. I made no sense to her; I asked her why people got married and she told me that I was no longer seven to ask such a silly question. That was a clear sign that my peaceful sunset tea was over and that I had to make a quiet exit.

So, why do women get married? To have a home, to have kids, to leave their parents' house, to start a life, to make love, to be responsible ...? This is so wrong! *Biological and physiological needs* like food, air, shelter, and sex, and *safety needs* like security, protection, and stability are at the very base of Maslow's hierarchy of needs. The need for *belonging and love* is midway between these two basic needs and the two superior needs of *esteem* and *self-actualization.* Looking at my aspirations now and my beliefs ten years ago, I can only be eternally grateful that I am not married to any of the men who came into my life.

A ten-minute meeting with an NLP guru six years ago changed my life. He asked me about what I was looking for in my Prince Charming and I innocently said: "I want him to make me happy." At the age of 25, I still believed in fairytales: a gorgeous man would stop me on the way to work, get off his horse, kiss my hand, kneel, point his magic wand at me, and order happiness to make itself at home in my heart. The NLP expert clapped twice, woke me from my beauty sleep, and told me that if I was not a happy person on my own, no one would make me happy ... ever! His words marked my memory and I slowly moved up Maslow's pyramid towards achievements, status, responsibility, personal growth, and fulfillment. Now I am facing a bigger problem!

In the movie Runaway Bride, Maggie Carpenter (Julia Roberts) asked Ike Graham (Richard Gere) if there was one right person for everyone, and he said: "No, but I think attraction is mistaken for rightness." I have been attracted to many people, but none of them felt right. There were always the ominous mental notes, the odd vibes, and the bad sparks. In my future vision of myself, I see kids and lots of fun, but no man ... I see myself as a single mom.

What is difficult about asking for a man with who I can have endless conversations? Who will be faithful? Who will hold my hand as we watch TV? Who will make me feel like the most beautiful woman on earth even when I feel like a shaggy doll? Who I know will come to my rescue whenever I call? Who will give me a knot in the stomach when I think of him? Whose name or number on my phone will draw a smile on my face? Who is my equal? Who appreciates my independence, cherishes my strength, and respects my weakness? Who is not some needy freak or disgusting creep? Who will let me be and love me for who I am? Is this too much to ask for nowadays? I am no princess so I no longer expect a prince!

Maggie Carpenter finally made it to the altar; she proposed to him by saying:
"Look, I guarantee there'll be tough times. I guarantee that at some point, one or both of us is gonna want to get out of this thing. But I also guarantee that if I don't ask you to be mine, I'll regret it for the rest of my life, because I know, in my heart, you're the only one for me." I will wear a ring and keep it, love a man and keep him, and get married and stay married, only when something in my heart tells me that he is the only one for me and that if I let him go, I will regret it for the rest of my life!

***

Avian flu gave us all quite a scare; we stopped eating chicken, set our colorful pet birds free, boycotted eggs and mayonnaise, and got ready for Doomsday. Then, like everything in life, it passed. We survived this one too – or so I thought, until I saw them at the pool. Men! Our very own Egyptian men got hit! Poor souls got infected by some sort of unheard-of virus that crawls into their tiny brains, fills their huge egos, and leaves 'junior' dangling like a small pendant to remind them, and us, of what was and what could have been. The ferocious infection causes them to abandon their guts along with their hunter instinct, and while they develop a crest and arch their backs, they greet the world with a dislocated chest, protruded behind, and a strut. Alas! What a sorry sight! They are under the illusion that they are peacocks!

I went to the pool with a group of friends and as we sat there enjoying the sun and ice-cream, I spotted a specimen of the weird breed across the pool. He stretched his arms, flexed his muscles, strutted back and forth, turned, and fluttered his ugly plumage at us. A minute later he was joined by another infected male who caressed his chest, adjusted his crest, and displayed his train of feathers. In an hour, there were seven of them strutting around the pool, graciously greeting one another, and looking busy and occupied with plenty of nonsense. They had their shades on, eyed every female at the pool, yet curled their lips as an expression of utter self-satisfaction and lack of interest.

The sun was in the middle of the sky and I had not gotten enough sleep the night before, thus making me susceptible to hallucinations. The loud, fake laughter coming from the other side of the pool echoed the noisy alarm calls peacocks make when they are trying to get the attention of peahens in the mating season. Their territorial calls, loud music, and peacock-ish attitude brought back memories of the stories my very scientific father used to tell me about insects, birds, reptiles, and mammals.

"The main purpose of the peacock's train is to charm the peahen to get her to mate with him. He spreads his train and displays an incredible fan of beautiful blues, greens, violets, reds, oranges, and yellows."

Like peacocks, the infected men acted as though they were pecking at food, with their heads to the ground and their tails above to draw attention to themselves. They were waiting for potential females to scurry over in the hopes of grabbing a meal, while they stood upright and enticed the ladies with their shining tails. Just as peacocks vibrate their tails rapidly at females in an attempt to impress them, the men across the pool shook their wings and tails from left to right as they coyly eyed us from behind their sunglasses. However, even with this awesome display, in the peacock world, it is very rare that we ever see them mate. The peahen usually pretends not to notice the peacock until she is ready to lay eggs, and only then will she decide to mate with the male.

In an attempt to get rid of this alarming line of thoughts, I got up and jumped in the water. My head definitely needed to cool off. But who was I fooling? One thought led to the other and Darwin took over. I was in biology class when I first heard of Darwinian Evolution. Darwin also observed that females are rather picky about their partners.

I never failed to see the basic rationale: random mating is stupid mating! The genetic quality of your mate will determine half the genetic quality of your offspring; ugly, unhealthy mates usually lead to ugly, unhealthy offspring. By forming a joint genetic venture with an attractive, high-quality mate, one's genes are much more likely to be passed on.

Coming back to earth from my Darwinian encounter, I watched a recently infected man with minor symptoms of peacock-ishness strut towards us. He greeted a common friend then he turned to me, uncovering a lovely pair of blue eyes and a very cute smile. I gazed back with mesmerizing green eyes that lit up a sun-kissed face, and the tournament began; table tennis with words, fencing with flirtatious moves, darts with penetrating smiles, and the usual wrestling matches. I was exhausted, he shed his feathers all over the pool, and the game was over. Like a peacock, he showcased his tail of feathers and talents, and waited for me, the female, to run in pursuit of his genetic qualities. But this female is fed up with the good-for-nothing peacocks; arrogant and stuck up for a bunch of useless colored feathers.

***

When I first watched *Silence of the Lambs*, I had a crush on Hannibal the Cannibal. Years later, when *Hannibal* was released, I grew to envy Clarice for the love of Dr. Lecter; I wanted to be her. Before you decide that I am a crazy chick, let me take you for a quick walk in my shoes. I have been in and out of many relationships that lasted from a couple of days to a couple of months. The ones that crashed before they took off did not last because the man in question did not exert any effort to get my initial attention, while the ones that crashed before they landed safely, ended because the man in question stopped exerting effort and took me for granted! They – Egyptian men – just do not want to work! I do not expect much; I just want to see a man going out of his way for me; what's the big deal? Shave his ugly head, lose a few extra pounds, get a job, wake up an hour early, sleep an hour late, drive an extra mile to see me, or any such thing that would translate into effort!

Now let me introduce you to the Dr. Lecter that I envy Agent Starling for: deep, intense, witty, handsome, and knows her like the back of his hand. He knows how her mind works and what makes her heart tick; he knows her every thought, fear, wish, and impulse. He loves her for her vulnerable strength. The beast had many chances to devour her, yet he declined. Hannibal Lecter dared her, challenged her, and pushed her from one limit to the other, but he was always there to save her soul when she gave in to despair. When the bad guys, society, enemies, or anyone hurt her, he was still watching over her shoulder; he hurt them for her. When it was his life or hers, he chose hers; when it was his wrist or hers, he saved hers; when it was his heart or hers, he broke his to mend hers. The beast went against his nature for her ... this is my definition of effort!

He called me Clarice and I called him Dr. Lecter, but I was no Clarice and he was no Hannibal. I was a bit taken aback by the fact that he was 14 years older than I was, yet I decided to give us a chance. I liked talking to him; he was smart, deep, and successful. As the sun set on his face, I saw glimpses of Sir Anthony Hopkins – I am not on anything, I am just blessed with an overdose of imagination. As we spoke, I wanted him to raise his voice a bit; his faint voice inspired neither confidence nor strength. His body language was that of a man who had given up on life somehow; the way his shoulders drooped, his legs slouched, his back arched, and his belly bulged made it hard for me to move beyond the age thing.

My friends accuse me of being superficial and hung up on appearances. They do not see him as that fat, or that switched off, or that old. "What's wrong with him?" they asked. Ladies, that question hurts so much; nothing is wrong with him, he is just not right for me. Why do you think that I should settle for less than what I want? Why do you think I should lower my expectations? Why do you deny me the right to be picky? Do you not think that I am worth it? Do you not see that I deserve it? Can I not do better? Am I that flawed? Am I that deluded? Are you that unfair? Thank you but no thank you ... Pass ... I will wait for as long as it takes.

Quid pro quo, my dear Hannibal – and that covers body, mind, and soul ... and he was never heard of again.

***

I lay on the white bed as my eyes moved back and forth between the monitor and his face. He was so quiet and tense and I could not understand anything from the images on the screen next to me; I had never seen the inside of my body before but from the look on his face, the doctor was not very pleased with what he saw. I summoned my courage and I asked in a faint voice what was wrong, but he replied vaguely that something was not right. He asked me a long list of questions, inquiring about things that I did, felt, saw, and wanted, then he handed me a long list of tests to be done, and asked me to come back in a month with the results. I looked him in the eye and asked if it was cancer; he looked away and said maybe.

I left the clinic with an odd mixture of feelings that ranged from absolute numbness to a merry-go-round of fear, anger, and warmth; I wanted to go home and hug my cats, call my friends, hit all my exes, hide in the closet, and, finally, I just wanted to cry.

After the initial shock, I decided to pull myself together and to think of how to deal with what the doctor had told me. In my very systematic head I began a thorough analysis of the situation where I eliminated, weighed, and accepted options. I made up my mind not to tell anyone, not to take the tests, and not to think of death. I decided to look at the bright side of this dark scenario and I chose to look at this as a wake-up call, not as a death bell. We are all going to die – there is no surprise here – but how we lived our lives is what will determine how we will feel about death. One thought led to the other and I found the missing part of the puzzle; the thought of dying did not bother me, but the thought of dying as though I never lived drove me crazy. I wanted to leave a legacy; to make a difference; to have some sort of an impact. Suddenly the anger and the fear that I felt earlier were gone and I was full of warmth; I was driven by a strong urge to share and to give.

The easy part was on the professional level; I decided to share my experience with young minds that are hungry for knowledge. I will leave a clear print on their present and future, and that alone gave me an immediate sense of satisfaction and a raison d'etre. I knocked on the right doors, said the right words, and got the right assignments to help me build my legacy. I built bridges of trust and respect that went beyond a classroom or a workshop. So whether I live a day, a decade, or a century I will know that I affected so many lives, touched many hearts, and shaped many minds. I know now that with my little words I made a big difference and my existence matters, will matter, and will have once mattered.

On the other hand, the relationship department suffered. I hit my head against one brick wall after the other; wrong people, wrong relationships, wrong intentions, wrong reasons, wrong decisions, and wrong expectations. This was the real vicious cycle that consumed my energy and my life. I had issues dropping the excess baggage that I had collected over the years; being judgmental, insecure, angry, aggressively defensive, defensively aggressive, stubborn, possessive, controlling, and indecisive. I also had issues keeping the men I liked and getting rid of those I did not like. I wasted a lot of passion on guys who were not worth it, yet I shunned away guys who needed it. My virtual receivers and senders had a mind of their own and my love life has always been a big mess. It took a lot of work and self talk to open myself to new horizons; basically to accept a partner who is not a cloned replica of me!

Finally I met Mr. Right. He is all I ever wanted and he brings out the best in me. He was there all along but I never paid attention. I automatically crossed him out because he is of a different religion … yes …. I forgot to add that to my wish list.

There are no absolutes in this life other than death. Forever is such an illusive word and I do not think that it has befriended anyone or anything; nothing lasts forever and no one lives forever; nothing is for sure and no one is certain of anything. No matter how far we go, we are always at square one; how many times will we have our heart broken? Who will we marry? Will we have kids? Will they be good kids? How will we live? Where will we live? When will we die? How will we die? Girls and boys meet up and break up every day and none of them knows who will take their virginity, whose ring they will wear, how many rings they will wear, whose babies they will have, who they will grow old with, and in whose arms they will die. So whatever I have or whoever I am with, I will enjoy it as long as it lasts and come what may. Speaking of absolutes, yes, he is not an absolute Mr. Right; but he is Mr. Right for right now.

***

At the end of a great day, I lay in bed with a peaceful smile on my face and dozed off. Suddenly, my heart was racing, my brain was pulsing, my breathing was heavy, and my eyes flashed wide open as the clock struck 12 midnight. It was now officially the 18th of September! It is his birthday; he just turned 33; I have known him for many years; his mother gave birth to him at 10:30 in the morning; he is a Virgo; he is tall, dark, and handsome; he is a successful marketer; he is witty, sarcastic, and funny; I loved him at first sight; it is over; it never started; I buried him and everything he stood for in a big soundproof box deep down in a forgotten corner of my heart and moved on. Why do I remember his birthday? Why do I have an internal timer with an awkward buzzer that goes off automatically every year on his birthday?

I met him on *one of those sites*. His replies were witty and cute. We exchanged emails and we began corresponding. I got attached to the emails; to the person behind the emails; to the mind who believed in the ideas in the emails. My imagination fed my heart with visions, my heart fed my mind with thoughts, and my mind sent shudders to my body – yes, I am saying that I loved him before I even met him.

After a few weeks we began chatting, exchanged pictures – I was wowed – and numbers. Our first call lasted three hours; there was no ice to melt; we just hopped from one topic to the other like best friends. We talked on the phone daily and the shortest call was at least an hour and a half; seeing his name on my mobile phone screen put an instant smile on my face; he talked about sports, job interviews, ex girlfriends, marketing scams, funny ads, movies, travelling, and many more topics. I have no recollection of what I talked about.

We fit our first date in between a funeral and an outing he had to go to. He called me when he was parked under my building; I flew down the stairs – five floors – and got in the car.

The memory of that day is so vivid in my head; he was wearing a black shirt and black pants, he had a lovely wide white smile on his face, he smelled of perfume and fresh laundry, and I had the most idiotic look on my face. I stumbled on my words like a blind man would stumble on garbage cans in the streets of Cairo. We drove around for a few minutes and I do not remember anything eloquent coming out of my mouth. He was looking at me and I wanted to hide from his eyes into his arms. He was talking, but I was trying to work on that stupid look on my face.

He drove me back, he learned that I live alone, he sent disapproval vibes, I replied back with pleading vibes, he decided to give it a half-hearted chance, and I was grateful. That was the first of many sleepless nights yet to come. I knew that I was blown away and I also knew that I left a very pale impression.

At the time, I had not yet mastered the arts and games that I know now; I still had an innocent, spontaneous little girl within. More calls followed and I got more and more attached; I thought of nothing but of being with him. I knew in my heart that we could have had the same vision for the future; that we could have had the best kids; that I could have made him a president with my strength and support. I wanted to love unconditionally and to give unlimitedly.

The list of the things he was not ready for and did not want did not need any sort of decoding. I knew that I was wrongly judged; I knew it was over; I knew I had lost him; I knew it was my fault; I knew I had to leave his house.

In a few months he developed some unheard-of allergy towards me. He could not stand talking to me on the phone, let alone seeing me.

After a series of failed attempts, I finally built my soundproof black box. I packed him, along with my feelings, in one dark black bag, I put the bag in the box, and I threw it in that forgotten place in my heart. Every few months he would sabotage my dreams, but I learned to live with that.

He became a faraway star high up in the sky; a star that I measure every man I meet against. I know very well that most stars shine from a distance but if you reach out and hold them in your hand, they are, at best, nothing but dull rocks, and, at worst, nothing but a piece of fire that can burn a hole into your palm, carve a grave into your heart, or turn your life into a living hell.
I got out of bed, reached for my phone, sent him a message wishing him a happy birthday, and hoping that next year he will be happier, wealthier, and wiser, and went back to sleep.

***

I closed my eyes and I saw a beautiful world; I was on Venus. It was a place that smelled good, felt good, looked good, tasted good, and sounded good - I was happy. Life on Venus was so healthy; we did not need to hunt, for we ate vegetables and fruits. We walked naked and felt great about our bodies. We had lovely little houses with cute little gardens. We spent the day grooming ourselves, talking, visiting, and enjoying the sun, the sea, and the fresh air.

Suddenly, all the women ran to the shore and screamed, "Alien"! A boat docked on our beach and out came a hairy, deformed creature that had ape-like features; his hair was tousled, his breath stank, he had fungus under his armpits and in other hairy places, his teeth had a yellowish-brownish tint, his eyes looked puffy and evil, his voice echoed the toads in the lake, he had a bulging belly, odd legs, rough hands, dirty nails, hairy ears, hairy nostrils, coarse skin, and an extra piece of meat that seemed so out of place. His manners were not any better than his looks; once he saw us on the shore, he began rubbing what seemed to be an itchy, dangling piece of meat, grabbing whoever was closest to him, invading our velvety world, and sweating like a pig. We were in shock, yet our caring nature forgave his ignorance and we made the mistake of our lives: we welcomed the outcast millions of years ago and are still suffering the consequences today.

My fellow sisters took him home, fed him, cleaned him, taught him manners, and gave him a home in our beautiful world. He slept, and the ladies took turns cooking for him, bathing him, grooming him, and caring for him. They took around-the-clock shifts to make sure that their guest was entertained and pampered. He began spreading his evil immediately and a month later, the ladies were competing over who would serve him, who would rub that itch, who would take him out, who would talk to him, who would stay with him longer, and eventually who would own him.

Our peaceful world was disturbed, we all lost, and he was the only winner. For the first time on Venus, there were friends who were not talking and ladies who were scheming against one another. The crime rate jumped from none to infinity. Curses and bad names replaced praise and compliments. Life on Venus changed forever.

One morning the alien, whom we named MAN, took a walk, and when he came back he was carrying a dead animal. He tore the poor thing to pieces and set it on fire. It smelled weird, but when MAN invited us to taste it, we could not be rude and turn down his invitation. We ate, we drank, and for the first time some ladies tasted meat; meat in their mouths and meat inside of them. They were cursed immediately; blood ran down their legs, morning sickness, bad temper, their bodies changed, and nine months later they were screaming in pain as a little creature came out of them. Being the nurturing creatures they were, the baby became the focus of their attention and MAN continued feeding more ladies with meat.

At times he called it food and at other times he called it sex, but for us Venusians they were the same thing. More ladies were cursed and Venus became MAN's home – and it all started with the damn piece of meat he fed us the day he went hunting.

One night MAN held a meeting and invited all the Venusians. After a few welcoming words, MAN started his speech by telling us that we should all be ashamed of ourselves; he threw a few leaves at us, asked us to sew them into something that would cover our ugly bodies, and called it modesty. We looked at ourselves and at one another, and suddenly we felt shame. We were crying as we gathered and sewed the leaves.

MAN began dictating his rules on our land and we obeyed him willingly. He called it protection. "Cover your bodies, stay home, cook for me, wash my leaves, clean my house, rub my itch, sow my seed, and say yes to whatever orders I give you," he said, and "yes master" we replied. MAN was smart; he convinced us that our land was no longer a safe place to live in and that if we ventured outside his territories or disobeyed him, all the mythical creatures would devour us, and we believed him – and it all started with the damn piece of meat he fed us the day he went hunting.

One morning MAN woke up and announced that only tall women were welcomed in his company; the tall women cheered and the not-so-tall women grieved. On another morning MAN declared his love for skinny women, and again all the chubby women exerted relentless effort to become skinny. He played the same game, and named it fashion, with the dark-skinned and the fair-skinned ladies, those with big bosoms and those with small bosoms – he even gave them ratings (A, B, C, D ...etc). He played us to his advantage and we were no longer happy with who we were. Our lives revolved around this one creature that had invaded our privacy and turned our inner peace into an eternity of hell. We experienced jealousy of one another; we coveted bodies and cast spells on souls – and it all started with the damn piece of meat he fed us the day he went hunting.

I thought that was the end of his tyranny until, in another meeting, MAN again told us that we should be ashamed of ourselves, and again we began crying immediately. He told us that we were possessed by the demon of lust and that we needed surgical intervention. MAN was kind enough to operate on us; he cut pieces of our bodies, claimed that it was in our best interest and called it chastity. Those who survived the trauma had one-on-one counselling sessions with MAN where he calmly guided our poor souls into utter submission and called it social code for 'good girls'.

His following commandments were basically that we, women, were the root of all evil and that our sexual desires were a curse. MAN stood tall next to a board and he carved the following letters into our traumatized minds: SIN; 'S' stands for Stupidity, 'I' stands for Ignorance, and 'N' stands for Nothingness. Months after repeating this lesson to cover all the female population, MAN no longer explained what SIN stood for; he just pointed his nasty, dirty finger at any one of us and said SIN to signify that she was stupid, ignorant, and a big nothing. We all sunk into a deep well of shame and guilt, and have lived there ever since - and it all started with the damn piece of meat he fed us the day he went hunting.

MAN died and many of the women I knew died, but one generation after the other still followed his teachings and applied his rules with avid precision. No one ever questioned them and no one dared disobey them. On another sad morning MAN Junior went to sea and he came back with a wicked, victorious smile on his face. Like his ancestor, MAN Junior got off his boat, women screamed, and he rubbed his itch, then he pulled a few women onto his boat, shackled their feet and hands, and we watched as his boat vanished into the deep blue. He came back a month later with the same ominous smile, no women, and what he called money.

More trips followed, more women disappeared, and more money was seen. The Venusians who were not sold when he went to sea stayed to serve him in a land that was once ours. We have descended from being goddesses and divas to being slaves and mistresses; we have been denied the right to any pleasure, as though we were created for the sole purpose of enjoying the delighted smile on the face of MAN Junior when we rubbed his itch or reaped his seed in childbirth. MAN Junior was a sexist by nature: if the seed blossomed into a Venusian, he called her a disgrace and killed her, and if the seed blossomed into one of his own kind, he called him pride and celebrated the newborn - and it all started with the damn piece of meat he fed us the day he went hunting.

I woke up with tears in my eyes - tears like the ones that have rolled down my cheeks many a time over worthless men. I know that the metal shackles are long gone, but I also know that our mindsets still believe that we are the root of all evil; that any woman who dares express her sexuality is a SIN; that men should decide how we dress, what we eat, where we go, and why we exist; that men dictate who is a bombshell and who is a nutcase; that men still use us to rub their itch and bring their seed to life; that men still label us and that we still submit to their judgment; that men still sell us, or buy us, in the name of marriage; that men still lock us in dark dungeons of fear of the future; that men still cut pieces of our bodies to deny us pleasure, and those who do not literally do it, cut pieces of our minds and common sense for the same purpose; that women still fight over men; that women still compete to please men; that women still bear the pains inflicted upon their bodies, minds, and souls by men - and it all started with the damn piece of meat he fed us the day he went hunting.

***

I met him and I was no longer angry at men. I had nothing more to ask Santa; he had finally found my perfect gift. I was flying somewhere between cloud nine and heaven. My moods depended on him. I did not want to waste a waking moment without being with him. Waking up in the morning felt great, going to bed at night felt warm, and life altogether felt different. I treasured every word he said to me, and passionately surrendered to him. There was always the ominous thought of a crash lurking at the back of my mind and ruining my best moments with him. I resisted my gut feeling and ignored my collective experience with 'his type of men'. I decided that this was a different man.

I would like to proudly announce that 'The Different Man' is a myth! He is a bigger myth than Santa Claus. There might be a Santa but there is no different man; they are all the same. Their names change, their faces change, their voices change, their bodies change, their geographic locations change, and their hunting styles change. But their hollow words, their void promises, and their bitter aftertaste are the same. I am at a point in my life now where I can safely assume that all men are the same; each man is an upgraded version of one of a few ancient models. Do not let their categories confuse you; they are ALL the same; they are ALL evil.

No matter how advanced or enhanced their software seems, they still share the same basic functions and manoeuvres. My relationship with men has become synonymous with knowing how a movie ends fifteen minutes after it starts. I told him that I have seen the movie Pay It Forward at least five times; I know exactly how it ends. Yet every time I watched it, the silly girl in me still hoped for a different ending. It was prewritten but still I hoped that some divine intervention would change the ending. I wanted him to prove me wrong. I wanted him to give me the different ending. But who was I fooling? I wanted him to last till

Christmas; I did not want another Christmas alone. But Alas! It is over!

I have reached a point where I am so familiar with the colors of sadness and madness. People say that each feeling is associated with a color. It is well known that red is the color of anger, blue of sadness, and yellow of bitterness. For some reason, these three feelings for me are all wrapped in a big brownish ball. Yes, the color of human waste - shit! This is the color that seals all my relationships; this is the word that echoes in the empty walls of what is left of my mind. I am sick of the color, the smell, the taste, and the feeling of deep shit! My heart is sinking, my soul is sulking, and a vicious crab is playing xo on my guts with its cutting edges. I am just sad; unfulfilled fantasies have a way of turning into nightmares, just as my Prince Charming turned into a frog. I know the drill by heart: sinking, sulking, aching, hitting rock bottom, then bottling it up, pushing it down, locking it in my black box with my other black memories, and then climbing my way up the tunnel.

Do I blame him? No. Am I angry at him? No. Do I want to smother him with the shit that is all over me now? No. I can't blame him. He said he would not hurt me, he said he was different, he said that I could trust him, he said that he felt at home when he was with me, he said so many things - but don't they all! Haven't I heard it all before? Why would that one be any different? Why would the ending change this time? Why did I believe this nonsense? I am at fault all the way; I was too spontaneous, very expressive, quite sincere, and literally blind. I did not make him earn my trust, I just handed it to him. I did not make him work for my company, I was at his command. I changed the way I did things hoping that the end of the story would change; I put my games, tricks, and spells aside when I should have kept them at an arm's length.

This was not my only mistake. My biggest mistake was going after a man who was in a relationship – a crashing relationship. I sat there like an ugly black crow waiting to prey on the remains of her heart. I thought I was a different girl. I thought he saw me as a different girl. What a deluded creature I am. I turned from the inspiration to the burden; from the muse to the block; from the comfort to the pressure; from the real thing to the distraction; from the relationship to the rebound. I hated him, then I hated myself; I was not sure whether to cry for his pain or mine; I decided to let go. I have broken my fingers, twisted my wrists, and hurt my arms trying to hold on to people who "had to" or "needed to" go away. I do not have the supernatural power of breathing life into dead relationships or people. I have been there and done that before – it is just another crash and it will pass.

I am trying to turn my back on the horrible feeling of being used; of being taken advantage of; of being taken for a quick ride; of being someone's painkiller. I want to close my eyes and not think of the intensity of the past few weeks. I want to wake up in the morning and remember nothing of him – or what could have been us. He was just another man among many others; another chapter in my book; another month in my life; another Christmas without a gift. There is no different man, just as much as there will not be a different ending.

***

"A man's character is his fate." — Heraclites, Greek philosopher (c. 540 - c. 475 B.C.)

After her father was shot dead, Clarice Starling went to live on a farm with foster parents. She ran away in horror when she witnessed horses and lambs being slaughtered. Their screams haunted her, and all her achievements, trophies, and honors were a relentless pursuit to silence the lambs. Mediocrity was the farm that I ran away from; my lambs were screaming for freedom and the wild horses within me wanted to feel the wind against their faces.

Back in 1994 I read Thomas Hardy's The Mayor of Casterbridge. The pessimistic novelist made it sound as though the hero's catastrophic fate was a natural by-product of his character. At the time, it all made sense and I fully agreed. Then one night I watched Return to Eden and I saw how a woman faced her worst fears, altered her self-perception, confronted the demons in her past, and changed how she talked, walked, and looked. She gave herself a new name and a new life. At the time, I did not like who I saw in the mirror and I resented the path that I was told to follow. I wondered if I could be someone else; would my fate change, were I to change my character?

It is amazing how much power we have, yet we are so oblivious to its existence. At home we were directed to focus on our downsides, at school we had to improve our bad grades, and in the workplace we are asked to develop our weaknesses. Those who have succeeded in aligning their character and their fate have done the exact opposite. I invested in what made me feel strong instead of wasting time on things that only made me feel weak and bad about myself. Marcus Buckingham says that knowing your strengths is the first step.

Stephen Covey tells you to "live out of your imagination, not your history." – This is the part where we get stuck; we do not believe in flying. We feel more secure with our feet on the ground, even if it is just quicksand. The most difficult step is the change itself. Change is an intrinsic part of our existence, yet we resist it to the bone. Dr. Spencer Johnson wrote in his bestseller Who Moved My Cheese?, that "if you do not change, you can become extinct." Fear always intercepts our attempts to change; fear of the devil we don't know; fear of the other side of the fence; fear of getting hurt or getting lost.

Over the years, I jumped one hurdle after the other. I managed to finally silence the lambs. To unleash the power within me, I turned my back on the little nerdish girl that I once was. I silenced the screams of the student who sat in the front row but always went unnoticed. The shy, frightened elf spoke up and earned her right to be heard. The little plain Jane Eyre has blossomed into a Madonna that is coveted for her uninhibited spirit and diversified career. I changed my character to change my fate.

***

To be or not to be! Hamlet!! I beg to differ! How much more limiting could that question be? How much more restraining could it ever get? Do we only have two possible answers to a question? Do we only have two things to choose from? Are our options so restricted? Are we so grounded? Have we gone color blind? When did our retinas stop seeing the colors of a rainbow? Why do we print our experiences in duotone? In a game of multiple choice questions, how many answers could be correct? What number of choices do we have? Who gives us the options? When do we have to submit our selections? Who decides if we passed or failed?

I was brought up to be your typical 'option-less' person, but I learned how to find micro-options and loopholes of choices in the tightest of situations and the trickiest of questions. It was always hard for me to choose between two dishes, or two men, when one gave me heartburn and the other made my brain go numb. I went through a long journey of self-discovery where I learned the virtue of the big picture, multi-dimensions, and different perspectives. I found my true calling and now there is no putting out the fire within my soul. It shocks me now to meet people who are still trapped in the narrow tunnels of low self-esteem and shackled to the ground by lead balls of fear. With their black blindfolds on, they face the brick walls of self-inflicted imprisonment and turn their backs to all the opportunities in the world.

We – human beings – have unlimited options. Choices liberate us, and knowing that we will never run out of options and alternatives is a relief. We are meant to choose. We are created to investigate options and alternatives. We are not equipped to compromise for the long term. There are times when we consciously limit our options because we do not want to feel overwhelmed by the infinity of choices out there. It is difficult to choose; the bigger the selection, the more helpless we feel. How do we know we are making the right decision? How do we know that we are choosing what is good for us? How can we tell that we are not going to regret this? Other than using our limited common sense and intangible gut feeling, we will never know!

Nothing justifies waking up in the morning hating what you wake up to, who you wake up with, or where you get up to go. Nothing explains leading an unfulfilled life with an unfulfilling job and an unfulfilling partner. We only live once, so we had better make perfect use of our time on earth.

I am not pleading for drastic measures like divorce, immigration, a great escape, or 180-degree career changes; I am defending our human right to choose. Our lives do not have to come to a standstill if we are in the wrong job with the wrong boss or in the wrong house with the wrong partner. We do not have to settle! We do not need to settle! We should not settle!

After being confined in a solitary cell, freeing your mind starts with knowing who you are. Find the answers in your heart: What do I like? What makes me happy? What makes my eyes light up with hope? What makes my cheeks glow with achievement? What makes me want to jump out of bed in the morning? What puts a smile on my face when someone, or something, rocks my boat? Be it a new language, a long-forgotten hobby, a dream career, a challenging sport, or anything else that adds flavor to a tasteless dish – anything that adds color to our black and white life. No, Hamlet, I am sorry; it does not have to be or not to be!

***

It was raining heavily and I do not like heavy rain. It was cloudy and grey and I do not like grey clouds.

It was windy and cold and I do not like cold wind. I put a few drops of cranberry fragrance oil in my burner and lit the tiny candle underneath, took my laptop in my arms, sat on the sofa, threw a blanket over my legs, and got online. I decided to browse Egyptian blogs and bloggers to see who is writing what. I typed 'Egypt' in the search box and I was redirected from one blog to another until I found his page. I do not know what made me stop and read; his words emitted a sincere and genuine vibe that blended well with the warming scent of cranberry that filled the room.

He was a typical Egyptian guy – not my favorite type – who had a typical Egyptian wife to whom he got married in a typical Egyptian way. They were leading a typical Egyptian life and they had no serious issues but for the every-now-and-then character clashes. She had a free-spirited genie locked within the bottle of the traditional Egyptian girl and she thought marriage would set the genie free. She pursued her love of nature in desert trips, safaris, and excursions, and he never understood her urges to sleep on the sand or to watch the sunrise from a boat. Nevertheless, they reached some sort of an agreement whereby she could have her breaks when he said that it was okay.

Gihan went blind; she lost her eyesight all of a sudden and the doctors said that it was a rare case. My eyes watered as I read Ahmed's lines: "My 25-year-old wife will never see the nature she loves again." He went on describing how she got depressed, shut him out, wanted a divorce, wanted him to remarry, quit her job, isolated herself, neglected her friends, and just gave up on life. There were a lot of tears between his lines and there were a lot of tears running down my cheeks. I could not even begin to imagine walking the famous mile in her shoes, or his. On her birthday he forced her to get dressed to go out and, to spare her the discomfort of being around people, he took her for a long cruise on a felucca.

Gihan asked Ahmed to lend her his eyes; she wanted him to tell her what he saw. He began talking about the scenery and she began asking him detailed questions. She wanted him to describe the sky; its shades of blue, the birds, the clouds, and the buildings on the horizon. She needed to know the color of the sun at that moment and he understood that orange is not a solid color. She asked him to tell her what he saw in the water and he learned the power of reflections. Gihan was the one who lost her sight, yet she was the one who lent Ahmed her eyes. For the first time he saw what she saw in nature and for the first time they enjoyed nature's beauty together.

His words came to a full stop and my day came to an end. Ahmed and Gihan were in my dreams all night, and when I woke up in the morning I did not jump out of bed. I did not run around the house trying to get myself in the car to go to the office. I sat in bed and smiled at my cats, slowly reached out to the curtains, pulled them away, opened my window, and watched the sunbeams smile back at me. Their light filled my room and their warmth filled my heart. I reached out to my cats and for the first time I felt their soft fur; before, I used to touch them, but that day I felt the warmth and the beauty of something that was beyond words – something that I took for granted.

What else did I take for granted? Who else did I archive unintentionally? What other signs did I miss on the way? What more could I not see? What did I never have the time to do because I was so busy? Who did I never have the time to meet because I had other priorities? I got a cup of tea, sat back in bed, and enjoyed a lovely new beginning to my morning. Eventually I got myself out of the house and drove to work; I decided to take a different route. I wanted to see new things and I reminded myself of how lucky I was to be able to look at such beauty. I am lucky to have the heart to enjoy it and I am blessed to be able to feel it. I am eternally grateful to Ahmed and Gehan – two people that I never met. The smile lasted that whole day, the day after, and many days that followed.

New beginnings are always loaded with many contradictory feelings; hope, fear, optimism, doubt, resolution, skepticism, comfort, hesitation, and determination. The skeletons in the closet and collective experiences are a threat to new beginnings. Regret, or the fear of regret, weighs heavily on our hearts as we try to embrace the sunshine. We remember when we were last burnt or when we were last hurt, and we subconsciously look at our scars. Memories of how deep and how painful they were rush back to our heads, and, with an involuntary movement, we clench our fists as though we are holding on to the past. Something inside of us refuses to let go and that very same thing resists the new beginning.

The tree will shed its old, dry, corrupted, infected leaves and will grow new, soft, fresh, green leaves. I will slow down and enjoy the drive rather than the destination. I will take off my masks, let my hair down, face the sun, smile, and breathe. I will borrow Gihan's eyes and, from now onwards, I will use them to carefully watch what I used to carelessly look at; to deeply look at what I used to superficially see; to simply see what I simply never saw. "Tomorrow is the most important thing in life. It comes in to us at midnight very clean. It is perfect when it arrives and it puts itself in our hands and hopes we've learnt something from yesterday." -- John Wayne

***

Being the daughter of an entomologist, I grew up playing with butterflies, examining mosquitoes, and studying the morphology of unheard-of flies under the microscope. One day my father got me a silkworm as a pet. With lots of love, I watched my worm transform into a cocoon and I waited for the colorful butterfly to come out of its silk hiding. I woke up one morning to find a small opening in my cocoon. I watched the butterfly trying to get out, then I decided to help her; I proudly, yet lovingly, cut off the remaining bit of the cocoon. The butterfly then emerged easily but something was wrong with my pet; it had an engorged body and small wings. I waited for the moment when she would fly. It never happened! My baby pet spent the rest of her life crawling. My dad then explained to me that the butterfly's struggle to get through the tiny opening was nature's way of strengthening my pet so that it would be ready for flying once it was free from the cocoon.

Today, as I watch many of the young men and women that I come across at work or in my classes and workshops, the image of my poor pet comes back to mind. I flossed my brains trying to find out the mental connection between the two until it hit me one day: in their attempt to protect their kids, mothers crippled them. "We want a revision," howled a 28-year-old marketing student in my class, but I see the pattern of the ready-made-easy-to-cook attitude everywhere. Like my butterfly, they face the world with shrivelled wings, limp bodies, porous bones, and hollow heads.

They are equipped to deal with neither the heavy blows of fate nor the daily challenges of life. They have no sense of direction and a vague reason for existence. Following the 'use it or lose it' rule of thumb, if they are not used, muscles turn to flab, brains turn to mush, and determination turns to lethargy. I loved my pet so much that I wanted to ease her way out of the cocoon but instead, I maimed her for life. According to Darwin, I turned what could have been powerful wings into a vestigial structure – like our degenerate tailbone and wisdom teeth. If nature allowed us to go through life without any obstacles, it would cripple us.

***

I was watching Matthew McConaughey and Sarah Jessica Parker's romantic comedy Failure to Launch, and I was highly entertained by the idea of working as an 'interventionist'. I would kill to get that job! Come on ... look at it my way - it would get me to date regularly and I would get paid for it! The plot was built around Tripp, a 35-year-old dude, whose parents were trying to get him to move out of the house. He had a nice job and a passion for sailing. His mother still made his bed, vacuumed his room, picked up his dirty clothes and left his clean laundry for him. She also made him pancakes, eggs, and bacon for breakfast. *Sounds familiar?*

At first I did not get the point of the movie – so what?! A single adult living with his parents – there is no law against that! Then I realized that in real life, with a subconscious twist, I have selectively dated men who live on their own. I also noticed that my resentment for guys who still live with their parents erupts in sarcastic comments, sudden mood swings, unjustified aggression, or implicit punishment sentences. Deep down I automatically consider them as less mature, less responsible, less reliable, and less worthy when compared to me. In that sense, I would be more experienced and more exposed than he ever was. I know this sounds awfully judgmental but this is how I weigh it.

It took a lot of strength and courage for a single girl like me to move out at the age of 28. Society, family, friends, men, and people who did not even know me frowned upon my decision. In the eyes of some, I was an outcast, for others I was insane, and for the majority I was a question mark. Five years later people still cannot understand my quest for independence and my need for growing into a whole person instead of becoming another female invalid who needs to lean on male crutches. I admit that leaving the nest has its pros and cons; the best thing about it is a sense of pride that only achievers can relate to. The worst thing about it is an utter lack of freedom. Yes! No freedom … responsibilities and bills govern almost every decision I make.

"To leave the nest, some men just need a little push," But what kind of push are we talking about when it comes to our men? How can we push a man away from his mommy's arms? How can we plant any seeds of responsibility in the souls of men who are so spoilt beyond reconciliation? Unlike parents here, in the movie, the parents were upset that their baby would not leave the nest; they felt that they had done something wrong in the way they had brought him up because he had failed to claim his independence. They hired Paula to motivate their son to move out. She believed that men still living at home lacked self-esteem, so she would establish a relationship with the man, build his confidence up and then move him out of his parents' house.

Let's assume that I got Paula's job. Let's assume that I am on a mission to throw men in the sea and that I will follow Paula's plan for launching a man. I would expect the following scenario: we meet by coincidence, he plays Mr. So-Big-So-Hard-To-Get, then after several manoeuvres from his side and some well-aimed blows from my side, he finally gets attached. I declare that our relationship will not progress until I know that he is an independent person who can survive on his own. Like other guys who are trapped in the comfort zone of their parents' house, he throws one excuse after the other at me and I brilliantly fail at my mission.

Excuses? Yes! Plenty! "My parents are too old. I have to take care of them and their needs. They will be heartbroken." Or "when I got married" or "people do not respect men who live alone, they automatically think that this man is a womanizer." Some are more honest and they just say that they are comfortable and well taken care of. Some say that the only thing they would miss about living on their own would be the ability to come and go as they pleased, and with whomever they pleased. One guy told me honestly that he could not afford it.

On the other hand, parents panic when their grown up little boy asks for his right to blossom into manhood. Somehow they interpret it as treason and ingratitude. They feel that they brought up an ungrateful little monster who walked away in their old age. Of course I will not start a girls-living-alone movement here; I am still fighting the battles of self-esteem with my fellow women. But men, our men, our macho men, our male prima donnas – why are they seeking refuge in the sheltered nest of mother goose? In nurturing societies like ours, independence is translated into aloofness and people living on their own are automatically categorized as troublemakers. Good boys and good girls never leave the nest unless they are dead, married, or forced to work abroad. Failure to launch … this is the one failure that families celebrate rather than lament!

***

If the producers of Beauty and the Geek wanted to torture someone who thinks of herself as a beauty by having her date any of those plain geeks on the show, then I would have made an excellent candidate. I am quite certain that those girls do not care about the geeks; they are in it for the money or the fame. I am also positive that they do not continue to date them once the cameras are off. With a pat on the head and a kiss on the cheek they send them off with their goddess-like smiles. Bottom line: the geeks are nice but they are not dating material! I cannot date Winnie the Pooh!

On her show, Ricki Lake invited some girls who were 'single by choice' and asked them about their physical requirements in a man. They all seemed to judge a book by its cover and have lost plenty of good guys to a fixation on physical attractiveness. Ricki told them that she had what they were looking for but the name of the game is a blindfolded date dare; the girls will literally go on a blind date! I admit that my eyes have always deceived me into choosing the jerk over the geek, but what am I supposed to do? Keep the blindfold on to maintain the chemistry?

So what is it that attracts me to, or repels me from, a man? I tossed away the character nonsense, the vision and mission clichés, and, by digging deeper into the layers of my Freudian heaven of a psyche, I narrowed it down to attractiveness! Yes! The attractiveness of a man is directly proportionate to my being attracted to him. Through extensive research, Dallas Barabasz-Lynn has been able to discern the inner structure of attraction. The Ladder Theory claims that 50% of a woman's attraction to a man depends on physical attraction, 20% on competition, 20% on novelty, and 10% on other things. Power and money were categorized separately; the amount of money, and the degree of power, required to get a woman's attention change according to her age.

In all my happy articles and sweet dreams, I envisioned myself with the tall, dark, and handsome prince; the captivating gaze, the broad shoulders, the flawless smile, the husky voice, and hard in the right places - *muscular that is.* I have a soft spot for long soft hair, breath freshener, clean laundry, and perfume. I also spot check nails and hands for cleanliness. Jerks who met these criteria made a doormat out of the little princess's heart – *yours truly*! Good guys who, in my eyes, had a weight or a shape issue were discarded immediately. Those who looked anything less than perfect were tormented to fit a mold that damaged me more than it hurt them. Those who were eager to please, I labeled as geeks, and those who accepted my inner or outer deformities, I crucified on the basis of their own scars and frailties.

The Ladder Theory points out how gals like me are attracted to competition; by competition, Barabasz-Lynn meant disinterest. The attractiveness of a man is by far stronger if he has other interests in life than making us happy. We are more tempted to pursue those who run away from us. What about novelty? Who wants an ordinary guy with a normal life and a normal job? – *boring … yuckkkkkk!* "Something different is more attractive. Like someone who does not have to work like most people because they have lots of money," says Lynn. I will add to that a few disorders that spice up the appeal of novelty: workaholic, alcoholic, manic depressive, obsessive compulsive, hypochondriac, malingerer, and chronic liar – *yes, I have seen it all!*

Moral of the story: if you are attractive, rich, powerful, novel, and show no interest in a girl, she is almost guaranteed to want to get intimate with you. Bonus points for destroying her self-esteem, flirting with her friends, cheating on her, and always being late, forgetful, noncommittal, manipulative, and controlling – *Isn't this the definition of the Alpha male? Isn't that the man who had the lion's share of my verbal, visual, and written curses?*

"So Beauty, why complain now of being painfully single, when you detest the jerks you have created and reject the geeks you have attracted?" asked the voice of reason that I so often silence!

***

"I am in an open relationship!" he said, like a proud Egyptian declaring his American passport.

"How do you mean?" I asked, like a poor Egyptian who has never seen a map!

I was not playing dumb; I seriously did not know what to make of his statement! Open relationship as in honest? No taboos? Creative? Mentally stimulating? Physically liberating?

He gracefully explained to my not-so-enlightened self that this was the ideal relationship because they would never get bored of one another, they got to enjoy space and freedom, and that he was open and candid about having other partners, but he would always come back to her. He asked me to loosen up because life was too short! He told me that he was very honest with his girl and with all the other girls; it was a sign of how decent and open-minded he was! *I walked away from the conversation before my violent streak took over, and ran to the comfort and warmth of my cats - who have so far proved to have better logic when compared to human beings.*

So an open relationship is like an open invitation for the man to come and go as he pleases? Who would accept that? Is it like permission to cheat? What kind of man would have the audacity to demand that? Does it mean that exclusivity is struck out of the context of the relationship? Why would anyone want to do that? So, could the girl have multiple partners as well? What would that make of her man? Half a man? If you delete commitment, trust, and respect from a relationship, what would you have left? Sex? Where would such an arrangement leave intimacy, bonding, and partnership? Why even call it a relationship in the first place?

In the old days, Egyptian men used to tell naïve girls that they were separated. I remember the first time I heard that line, I asked a series of closed-ended questions for clarification; I always started with whether they lived in separate houses, and when the answer was negative, I asked whether they lived in separate bedrooms, and when that test came out negative as well, I would ask timidly if they slept in separate beds. Most of the time, that also was negated. I used to struggle as I asked for a definition of being separated, and I was always told that they were separated on the mental and emotional level. *This is my definition of sliced baloney marinated in crap that men feed us all the time!*

A decade later, men have grown wiser and realized that their "I am separated" line is not flying. They used the head on top of their shoulders and voila: a new type of relationship that sounds so politically sound - an open relationship was their proposition! A solution that relieved them of any previously felt guilt. He does not have to lie about his whereabouts or hide his tracks anymore; why should he when his partner gave up her right to *object* and agreed to become an object in his life? There are two types of girls who would accept such a deal: Prototype A is a girl who does not have true feelings and is using him just as much as he is using her. Prototype B is a desperate girl who consensually gives the man the right to kick her behind whenever he pleases. Aside from the traditional code of ethics, and, shockingly enough, I carry more respect for the first type, as opposed to contempt, with no traces of sympathy, for the second, I have nothing against open relationships - if they are really open relationships - but when it is another excuse for the guy to fool around then it is worth writing about.

***

I am about to advocate something that I have never believed in. Actually, I am on the verge of stabbing a deeply rooted belief in our multi-layered culture. The same girl that, given a chance, would have poisoned every man or woman who accepted getting into an open relationship - that very same girl - is about to cross out monogamous relationships and validate having multiple partners. To save face, I will refer to monogamy as 'vertical relationships', and 'horizontal relationships' are to be synonymous with polygamy - I am still having psychological barriers with the word!

Let me start by defining the two terms. Vertical relationships mean that you are in a relationship with one person whom you get to know, understand, appreciate, and love over time. This is a type of relationship that involves a lot of trust, dependability, possessiveness, and depth. If you are in a vertical relationship, you invest deeply and seriously in the relationship and in the partner - you put all your eggs in one basket, so to speak. If that basket falls, your losses are countless. 'Your eggs' in horizontal relationships are randomly distributed in several baskets; you do not place all your bets on one horse and your investments are diversified to secure you from bankruptcy. Horizontal relationships are neither fake nor superficial; they are just not deep enough to cause serious damage should someone try to pull your tooth out.

Like my multiple careers, I began juggling multiple partners. I have always complained of the scarcity of good men, yet I found myself attracted to several men at the same time. They have nothing in common but me. I have grown to like them as individuals and to appreciate what each one has brought into my life. The intensity that used to ruin my previous vertical relationships was working in favor of my horizontal relationships. To the four, I was never too available, too focused, too critical, or too demanding, simply because what one man lacked another fulfilled and I felt loved and cared for all the time. Moreover, when one man slouched, instead of reprimanding him, as I used to, I would just give more room to the others to fill in the void that was left behind.

But before you go ahead and embark on one of those awesome horizontal relationships, you need to know the pros, the cons, and the rules. I have spent enough time analyzing my experience and I will gladly share with you my findings. On the upside, you will never need to depend on the presence or absence of one person in your life. You will never feel lonely, bored, hurt, insulted, or cheated, and you will never have to spend another weekend alone. You will always have a date, and, worst-case scenario, you will always have an email, a text message, or a phone call to put a smile on your face. You will never look like a famished Somali kid in front of an open buffet. Basically, you will be happy! On the downside, if you are not the organized type, you will suffer stress, overlapping schedules, exhaustion, and the wear and tear of your mind trying to cope with the constant change. If you are the melancholic type, you will long for the intimacy that builds up in vertical relationships. If you are the committed type, this will not work for you!

But if you want this to work, you must abide by the rules. Honesty is the first and foremost of all the rules; never lie about, or hide from, the fact that you are having multiple partners. Do as you would be done by – you are still an ethical person who does not step all over people in the name of horizontal relationships. Do not promise exclusivity when that is not the case. The second rule is an extension of the first rule: do not claim to enjoy horizontal re-lationships hoping to entrap a vertical partner. This strategy is doomed to backfire.

The backbone of this type of relationships is to truly, genuinely, and sincerely like your partners – all of them. This is not as easy as it sounds. Most of the time, people who are used to vertical relationships would like one partner and line up the others to fill in his shoes in case of absence or misconduct. This strategy is fatal; being with people you do not like, or with people you like half-heartedly, will push you back forcibly into the arms of the one partner you like – and we all know how being clingy is inversely proportionate to being loved. Horizontal relationships are a great illustration of how the sum of the parts could be bigger than the whole; each one of your partners alone would make a wrong partner, but together their weaknesses seem to vanish with the sense of perfection they bring into your life.

I have always pleaded for equality, and it is only fair to remind you that you are free to come and go as you please and so are your partners. Every now and then you will feel a tingling sense of jealousy towards one of your partners but it is never as suffocating or as painful as the jealousy you feel towards your sole partner in vertical relationships. Were there a 'flirting nerve' in our body, then this is the type of jealousy that triggers it. Horizontal relationships are, so far, liberating, fulfilling, pleasant, and they add a different flavor to each day.

***

When did I become so class conscious? How did I grow into that obnoxious girl that categorizes people based on where they live, what they wear, and how they talk? Their dialects, education, and possessions determine their location on my social stratification model. I am not materialistic by any means – I just believe that social class reflects on a person's general disposition in life: occupation, education, qualifications, income, grooming, manners, cultural refinement, taboos, and language and diction. I fully realize that over the years, I have evolved from a common middle class girl into a distinguished lower-upper class lady.

In 1949 William Lloyd Warner set an early example of a stratum class model: upper-upper class is what we call 'old money', and those are people who have been born into and raised with wealth. Lower-upper class is equivalent to 'new money', and those are people who, like me, have become rich within their own lifetimes and due to their own work. The upper-middle class is like my family, professionals with a college education. But other members of my family belong to the lower-middle class, who are low paid white collars, but not manual laborers. Today, I believe it is only fair to mingle with or marry from my current social class.

Ok ... let me start from the start. It hit me for the first time when I met Lisa in her office back in June 2001. She was leaving Egypt and I was her successor. I still remember how my eyes wandered around and literally fell in love with everything Lisa had in her office: the glass bowl and goldfish, the scented candles, the tall vase and bamboo shoots, the lace curtains, the Christmas cards on the shelves, the pink and orange pens on her desk, and his picture - a picture of a dark Egyptian man on Lisa's desk.

"Ismail, my husband," Lisa said, and I did not know what to say. He obviously looked like an impoverished under-educated working-class Egyptian. As though Lisa could read my mind, she openly admitted that he was poor, that his English was even poorer, and that his family was among the poorest, and that she knew that I would never consider talking to him, let alone getting married to him. I was shocked and perplexed. I struggled for the right words and nothing came out.

Later on that day, Lisa told me that her mother thought she was out of her mind when she decided to get married to Ismail - a black Arab waiter who could not speak English. But she had never met a man who made her feel so special and so precious. She did not need him to talk to her in English, when everything she needed to know was written in his eyes. I told her that they were different – socially and culturally different. She replied with confidence that we were all different and that if I was looking for a man who is a clone of me, then I would look for an eternity – in vain.

I told her that she was smart, pretty, successful, well educated, well traveled, and well positioned in her career. She could have had any man she wanted. Lisa's smile grew wider as she told me that she did get the man that she wanted. She told me that people from the same country might share the same cultural outlines but when looking deeper one would find various sub-cultures, norms, values, and beliefs. Lisa told me that she loved his family; they had a small house, yet they insisted that she spend a few days with them. They had little food, yet they shared it with her. They did not speak her language, yet they made her feel welcomed and important with what went beyond words.

"Why do you insist on turning human beings into dogs who have to wear collars and labels to identify them?" Lisa's words still resonate in my head and I still have no answer.

***

I cannot deny that there are times when I wonder how my life would have differed had I not called off my wedding. If I woke up on the right side of the bed, my thoughts took me to a cozy house with a loving husband and lovely kids; but if it was one of my countless bad hair days, I envisioned a miserable wife in a boring marriage with teary-eyed kids, and sleepless nights contemplating a flawless murder. I am certain that had I married the guy who used to exercise his 'stick', or the guy who wanted to deliver his own babies, or the alcoholic, or the neurotic, or the psychotic, or the caveman, or any other guy, I would have been divorced. I do not think I would have made it past the first month, let alone the first year. I was miraculously saved, but many young Egyptian couples were not as lucky.

What fed their dreams to the shredder? What turned their vows into curses? To love but not to hold? For the better but not for the worse? For the richer because no one wants the poorer? In health but never in sickness? What would make a young bride run away from the love nest? What would make Prince Charming flee on his not-so-white horse? Was it a bad choice? Was it that marriage put an end to the dating farce? Is it the lies? Is it the false pretences? Could it be expectations? Could their premature divorce be the only natural outcome of the marriage of a couple who were incubated in a schizophrenic society? Am I being too pessimistic? Am I being too realistic?

We are victims of our society. The double standards that we are brought up to adopt create, what we call in business, an execution gap. There is a big void between where we really are and where we want to be; what we want and what we have; how we feel and how we act. We drown in an abyss of deluding illusions, unrealistic expectations, fake emotions, consuming demands, and the inevitable frustration. We get married for the wrong reasons; we mistake lust for love and confuse stability with stagnation.

Mothers are over-protective as though they want to suck us back into their wombs. Fathers discriminate between their sons and daughters. Women sing to the deaf ears of their male counterparts. Men play to the sensitive tunes of female vulnerability. Traditions, manners, taboos, and religion mix in one melting pot that defines stereotyped outlines for our ideal character and our perfect mate. We are dictated the answers to all the quizzes but we are left to face the final tests alone – we fail with flying colors.

***

Relationship Warning: Do not get involved with Egyptian Men!

Because of the nature of my work in the tourism sector, I am used to hearing that this or that country has issued a travel warning to its citizens who plan on traveling to Egypt, especially in the aftermath of an attack. Naturally, most warnings address safety and security issues, and some warnings dedicate a section or two to hygiene and harassment. Lately, and because of the increasing number of divorces, custody issues, and domestic violence cases, some countries warn their women against Egyptian men. Yes, they tell them clearly not to get emotionally involved or legally committed to an Egyptian man!

I did not just make that up. I got it first hand from a European woman who is living in Egypt, was married to an Egyptian man, has a son, and is currently divorced. "He swept me off my feet with his sweet words, compliments, attentive gestures, romance, and warmth; he was a god compared to European men, who are often distant, reserved, and not very emotional. I fell in love with him like never before. Bit by bit, I began opening up too and, against my better judgment, I gave up all my defenses. In three months, he asked me to marry him, and in my culture this is a very serious step. I translated his proposal as the epitome of love and I gladly accepted."

I listened to Sue and I knew exactly how she felt when she first met 'her hero'. I know how it feels to jump into a jar of honey thinking of how sweet it would taste and how rich and overwhelming it would feel, only to get your hair tangled in its stickiness and eventually you drown in its suffocating viscosity. I asked Sue to continue narrating her experience and she told me that his family was against the marriage. "They told him that I was loose and that he should get married to a virgin. They warned him that I would corrupt his children and reminded him that I was from a different religion. His mother hated how I dressed, no matter how modest. All my attempts at communication failed, but I was too heads over heels in love with him to read the warning signs. He assured me that he loved me and that he was not willing to give up his soul mate."

Her eyes welled as she told me her story. I tried to be as empathetic as possible, but I was growing angrier by the minute. I naturally assumed that her guy was a lowlife Egyptian male parasite who wanted a way out of the country or easy sex. Because un-Egyptian women are not as class conscious, they miss out on all the 'low-class' signals that his body language, address, grooming, verbiage, phonetics, and interests give away. I was wrong! "He is an AUC graduate and the descendant of one of the biggest families in Egypt. He had the looks, the manners, the class, the charm, and the money. He was so open-minded and understanding – I have never met anyone who was as perfect," Sue corrected me.

I was more than curious to know what could go wrong with such a compatible intercultural union. "We got married amongst his friends. His family did not attend but this was natural in my country; we were two responsible adults and we were in charge of our life-altering decisions. After marriage, he began changing; suddenly he had hurtful comments about my wardrobe, more hurtful comments about my public demeanor, and … he hit me! He told me that he loved me but suddenly his love began suffocating me. I realized that I got married to a very jealous, possessive, insecure, spoilt, violent person!"

Again I identified with every word she said. I KNOW our men! I asked Sue about the frequency and the intensity of the jealousy fits and the violence attacks and she told me that it became on daily basis. "The tender, loving, caring man that I fell in love with disappeared. I was stuck with a person who mastered ignoring me, and when he looked at me, he told me that I was ugly and needed plastic surgery." With her long golden locks tied back in a ponytail, Sue was looking at me with deep blue eyes that rested on pink cheeks. She was flawlessly pretty! But I am fully aware of the self-esteem blows that our men know how to perfectly aim.

After a year of suffering and utter misery, Sue got a divorce … and a son! Being a single foreign mother in Egypt could be quite traumatizing. I asked her why she did not go back to her country; she told me that her Egyptian god had threatened to take away her son. To add a more dramatic denouement to this repetitive farce, Sue told me that after their divorce, he remarried and that he stopped sending her alimony. This was when she went to the embassy and that was when they told her "we told you so!"

Just writing about this topic clogs my arteries; I have witnessed many other stories that started with "he was so sweet" and ended in "I hate Egyptian men." Even the girls who were spared the marriage disaster still enjoyed a rough ride on the dating arena. Sue told me that her countrymen could still bully their women and that they were far from perfect, but at least they were honest, straightforward, and took marriage seriously. Like many Egyptian girls, she felt that he cheated his way into her heart and that he tricked her into loving him. It was ironic though, how Sue thought that Egyptian women were best equipped to deal with their men.

***

Sitting on a stone couch on the terrace of my soon-to-be home, I grew wings and soared high into the horizon. I enjoyed the sunset as the scent of orange blossoms filled my heart with joy and birds sang their prayers to a new dusk. A sense of achievement flowed through my veins and a happy tear twinkled in my eyes as I embraced my future. My mobile rang. She was a friend. I answered. After a stream of courteous greetings, my friend asked about my whereabouts, and I informed her that I was checking the paint colors at my new apartment. I embarked on an infinite rant about the beauty of everything I laid my eyes on until she caught me off guard with a question: "Will your boyfriend move in with you?" I met her question with silence, followed by a need to go and do something!

I was not offended by her question; I was just baffled – needless to say, clueless. First, I was not sure which boyfriend she was referring to. Who has she seen me with? Who have I told her about? Who has been in my life long enough to be a boyfriend? Who does she think I love enough to share a home with? I honestly could not pin a face to her question. The second and main source of my confusion is the fact that I have never given that particular issue any thought. It is true that I have been living alone for the past five years, but I have never considered it 'home'. It was as though I borrowed someone's car; I have to keep it clean, keep it safe, treat it with respect, and return it on time in perfect shape.

Now I own a home and one day I will have a boyfriend who will make it past the first month. What if he makes it past the first six months? It is one thing to come and visit and it is a totally different thing to move in with me. Bearing in mind that I am a very territorial person – territorial enough to pee all over my desk so no one would dare sit on it – and bearing in mind that I value space and privacy beyond any man I have ever known. Will I be willing to share? Will I welcome his clothes in my wardrobe? Will I be able to see his toothbrush next to mine in the bathroom? Will he have a key? Will he really move in with me?

Other than my space issues, there is a lot of social baggage that comes with such a situation. Like losing your virginity, abortion, homosexuality, and extramarital affairs, cohabitation is another taboo in our society; for a couple to live together they have to be married. They get to really know and understand one another after they are legally bound to one another - another instance of burying our heads in the sand and sweeping our dust under the carpet. I believe that this is a major factor that is ruining all my marriage and commitment attempts. Between cultural variations, personal differences, and individual perks, I find the idea of cohabitation rather appealing and logical.

When two people come together, they are not just who they are today; they represent their respective homes, schools, friends, peers, and groups with their attitudes, habits, beliefs, and needs. This is a lot of ironing to do in a relationship. How a person eats, talks, or walks is just the tip of the iceberg. The way one communicates with, reacts to, and feels about things and people is a wide enough gap to bridge. Hence, many love stories crash after marriage because he was not who she thought he was or because she was not the girl she said she was.

The idea of sharing is in itself frightening; who is to do what? Assigning roles and responsibilities and trying to fulfil them over a long period of time is like the prologue to a marriage. Is he responsible? Is she reliable? Is he stingy? Is she a control freak? Is he too organized? Is she beyond sloppy? There is no other way to find out. Living with someone is not just about the sexual part of the relationship; it brings out the mental and emotional dimensions to the foreground and the day to day dealings are the real test of the success or the failure of the relationship.

Moving in together does not mean that one partner is hosting the other at his home – responsibility free. I am walking the whole nine yards here; electricity, water, gas, maintenance, food, and the rest of the bills. I am speaking about chores, tasks, duties, compromises, and adapting. How hard would it be for a man to move into my house and be reminded every second that this is 'my house' and he is not entitled to anything? How hard would be for a woman – who is not me – to live with a man who treats her as a guest? How hard would it be to discuss the money issues and the other 'embarrassing' issues? – I assure you it is much harder to talk about those things for the first time after the deal is sealed and signed.

I am also not claiming that jumping that hurdle is a guarantee that the relationship will last forever. People change and people grow in different directions; a couple could live together happily and get married, then after a year or two they could grow apart. Keeping a marriage intact is another story and it takes a lot of work on a different level; fighting redundancy and boredom that creep into the marriage requires two people who want to stay married and are willing to work to reap what they once sowed. In a way, it is much easier to reach the highest top than to stay on top.

I am not advocating brothels and turning one's home into a full board motel; I am talking about a relationship that has grown and has developed into something solid and is worth investing in. At the same time, I am not promoting the notion of test driving the man; I am pushing the idea of test driving the marriage concept to that man. Having thought about it now, the 'living together' phase is all good; if it works, then you will have a solid marriage with no nasty surprises because of how she looks when she wakes up or how he sounds when he goes to sleep. If it does not work, then you have saved yourself a rough marriage or an inevitable divorce.

***

Was I bored? Maybe! Was it loneliness? Possibly! Was I hurting and in need of a quick fix? Maybe all of that and more! It was just one of those insane moments where one consciously decides to break a rule for the heck of it. I typed the address of the world's largest sex & swinger personals community in the browser box and waited for what seemed like an eternity before I clicked the 'go' button. The homepage featured a clip of a semi-naked babe dressed in almost nothing, and her eyes seemed to stare back at me as though she was challenging me to actually do it.

I was too intrigued to walk away. I accepted the webmaster's invitation to create an account – actually, I created two. For my female account, I came up with a super sexy name, ripped an extra seductive picture off the net, wrote a state-of-the art introduction about myself, filled in the required fields, and submitted my form. I went through the same steps to create my male profile, but the name and the picture were more inspiring. I took shelter in a foreign name; Jenny and Mike were the names I used when I talked to people. Immediately, I received a congratulations email and my passwords. I was all set to go.

The first logical place to start was definitely browsing the profiles of other members to get an overall idea (209,749 listings in Egypt). Then it was only natural to start searching the profiles based on my personal preferences: country, age, gender, hair, eyes, body type, endowment, bedroom interests, marital status, fantasies, desired type of relationship, and other options. I decided to go for four basic searches in Egypt:

men looking for women, men looking for men, women looking for men, and women looking for women. The handles (nicknames) were not very encouraging and the headlines were even more discouraging, but whose words was I expecting to read?

I also visited this site's affiliate sites specializing in alternative lifestyles, Asians, Russians, Literotica, and BDSM (Bondage and Discipline, Dominance and Submission, Sadism and Masochism). I was amazed – Egypt had a very strong presence. After a week, when the site realized that I was not going to pay, yet I was attracting a lot of members, they gave me access to all profiles, and I was able to contact whoever I fancied. I tried to be as selective as possible without limiting my options. I sent emails left and right, driven by curiosity and my own emotional issues.

The messages I received from men were - at best - revolting. I nearly cried when I read the first email. The female in me felt assaulted by a few words describing her privates and what this complete stranger wanted to do to her. I toughened up over time and I learned how to just ignore such emails. I also learned to keep my lower jaw in place when I was sent phone numbers, nude pictures, or more intimate pictures.

EgyptHorse, Confidant, Rambo, FireBird, MaadiMan, SexyMan, and Funny_Pilot are examples of men looking for women for various purposes – be it one-on-one sex, group sex, erotic chats, exhibitionism, voyeurism, or swapping and swinging. Feline Wolf is a Lebanese man who comes to Cairo regularly on business; he was looking for "an escort". Sinner is an Egyptian looking for a "no strings attached" relationship because he does not want to go through a third divorce. 54-year-old Akhnatun is interested in erotic chats and sharing pictures.

While Domination Nature is a man who finds pleasure in using whips, needles, and candle wax, Undisciplined Boy needs a firm mistress. Married men had various reasons: Firestarter feels that he cannot share his fantasies with his wife because "she made fun of him". Hawk feels the he has stamina for more than one woman as "this is how God created men". Gringo does not feel appreciated by his wife who "never initiated sex". Nile King is not interested in marriage; he can get all the sex he wants without the responsibilities of marriage, and Sex king is a businessman who throws regular group sex parties "for business and pleasure".

The male version of me was much luckier; most of the emails were of a gentler nature. Moonlight is looking for women in Cairo for "warm passionate sex" and Female_Touches is inviting women and couples (two females only) to check out the "things in (her) for a female's touch". Many of these girls were looking for a relationship not a one-night stand. There were girls who were impoverished enough to ask for money or food in return of their services! A girl advised me to put on a veil for more discretion. "This is how I ensure that the guys I got intimate with did not recognize me outside the bedroom," she explained. Wanna_FuninBed, Nana, Sex_Teen_Secrets, Sexy_Lady, AreULove-Pussy, Nouny, Maya, Dala3ny, and Salwa seemed so real yet so desperate. Their invitations ranged from a simple "I love sex", to more particular requests, attention to certain body parts, and less conventional forms of sex ... got it?

Candle Light is a virgin who thinks that it is okay, religiously and socially speaking, to have sex with a girl. Hot2handle is a lesbian who has had it with men; "I have been hurt so many times. I can't take it anymore. I will never understand men." Mooneye is a married woman who feels neglected and totally unsatisfied; "I feel invisible and it hurts." Ranrona is bisexual and wants to have sex with anyone who promises to keep her virginity. Romance Chance is engaged and cannot let her fiancé kiss her but she has no problem sleeping around: "I already have a hymen restoration procedure in plan". Hermoso is a divorced woman who does not want to get married again.

Narnar is a man who pretends to be a woman to hunt easier. My masculine picture also attracted a few homosexuals who shared the memories of their first time, their expectations, and their fears. AlwaysBottom, Beast, Frankie, and Migos are males seeking other males. Egy-Sub is a young boy of 24 who needs to be dominated by men and Femboy is a cross dresser who has a list of "cross dresser parties in Cairo".

The homosexual or bisexual girls who contacted me were mostly men in disguise. Some of them were girls who were sent on a hunting mission by the men in their lives – a threesome was their demand. Out of boredom, dissatisfaction, and experimentation, couples were willing to host me at their homes; women wanted to share their men and men wanted to share their women. Bi4Bi is a couple who needs a female companion. CoupleforLove are two girls who want to play with another couple. Egycouple are a couple looking for a man to please the woman in the presence of her husband.

I will neither get on the pulpit to preach the morality or the immorality of adult dating sites, nor will I point fingers at the people who, at one point of time, were my friends and support group. I just want to share and document my personal experience in a world that changed my life forever. My fake foreign identity made it easier for both genders to open up to me. They easily talked about their expectations, needs, and fantasies and I had a microscopic view of the rotten corrupt cells that are eating up the roots of our once intact society. I have always known that we were plagued with frustration, but I never realized how deep or how far it went. I was confronted with the ugliest faces of double standards and hypocrisy.

I have mixed feelings about my adventure: shock, awe, curiosity, shame, and disdain towards the sites, the people on the sites, their activities, and my involvement. Instead of facing our problems and ailments, we escape to a fantasy land of our own creation. These people are neither fiction nor the inhabitants of a faraway land; they are Egyptians living with us and among us. Some of them are well established members of society and carry the burden of family names that open closed doors. Others are soliciting prostitution in their own ingenious way. They are our neighbors, colleagues, and role models; souls trapped in bodies that they hate and in lives that they resent; hidden personalities that lead secret lives, escaping to the forbidden underworld, to the world beyond firewalls.

***

"Let me give you a little inside information about our society; our society likes to watch. It's a prankster. Think about it. It plays on man's instincts. It gives you extraordinary gifts, and then what does it do? I swear for its own amusement, society sets the rules in opposition. Look but don't touch. Touch, but don't taste. Taste, don't swallow. Ahaha. And while you're jumpin' from one foot to the next, what is it doing? It's laughing its sick head off! It's a sadistic society!" – That was me playing John Milton in Devil's Advocate! What was it this time that offset my safety valve? Was it a guy who started the lame, nauseating right and wrong argument with me? Was it a girl who hid her actions in a cloak of virtue and self-righteousness? Was it a married couple who preached what they never practiced when they were single? Regardless of what irritated my hyper allergic brains, the fact remains that we are a shame-based society nurturing a guilt-based culture.

'Shame' – what a word! It has the power to clog your mouth and seal your lips just by pronouncing it. Have you ever noticed how such a tiny word can lock your mind, inhibit your feelings, and imprison you in a world of rules that are not supposed to be broken just because it is a 'shame'? We were born free and uninhibited, and then we were given 'the rules of shame and its derivatives': cover your body, hide your feelings, withhold from expressing your opinion, and filter your words before you get yourself in trouble, were all tips to treasure from childhood onwards.

In the presence of her family, a girl would curl her lips and condemn others who 'shamelessly' hold hands with their boyfriends. In the company of his friends, a man would brag of dumping a girl for 'shamefully' offering herself to him. On a shopping spree with her mom, she would show her resentment towards a couple kissing inside the elevator. They all want to belong; they all want to be accepted. This is why we lie, fear judgment, and wear masks and faces to hide our own. The question is: who do we see when we look in the mirror?

We are sucked into a black hole of contradictions where human termites are eating away our uninhibited essence and our basic human rights are vacuumed by the hands of society and its code of ethics. On a scale of shame from one to five, one being the least shameful and five being the most shameful, kisses scored the lowest and full intercourse scored the highest on a list of physical actions between a girl and a guy who were not married. Touching with clothes on was more acceptable than making out naked. External sex is less grave than penetration. Why? Because what the eyes do not see the mind does not judge and what you don't know will not hurt you – hail thee ostrich land!

I asked four families who were not related if they would let their daughter date. They unanimously said no; but, one mother said that if her daughter was seeing someone, she did not want to know about it. One of the fathers said, with a stern knowing face, "She is not a boy." Another mother said she knows that her daughter has a boyfriend but "thinking that I do not know, will make her feel guilty. When she feels guilty she will not make mistakes."
Couples and singles were asked to explain their boundaries; what will they do and what will they not do. Nahla and Amr said that they would do whatever pleased them because they were in love. Their families did not know and if they broke up no one would know. Samar and her boyfriend said they moved in together but told the doorman that they were married. Rehab said that she always kept him wanting her but she denied him anything that went beyond holding hands. Her significant other had a smile on his face as he told me that this was why he trusted her. He knew for sure that he would be her first and last. Mona does not let her boyfriend touch her at all but she "has a few guys stashed for *'touchy-feely'* purposes."

Omar would never take a girl's virginity, even if she asked for it. Tamer promised that the girl would walk out of his house just as she walked in; "if she walks in a virgin, she walks out one, and if she walks in not a virgin, she never walks out pregnant". Hisham told me that there were wives and there were whores; a whore would never be marriage material. I had to ask him to define a whore; he said he was referring to loose girls who wore bikinis at the pool. "If I am with her, she would let me rub oil on her body and touch her all over. How could I get married to one of those?" Khaled said that he would never get married to a girl who was known to have lost her virginity. I naturally assumed that he wanted to get married to a virgin until he said, "but if it is a secret and no one knew, I could forgive her and marry her." I was perplexed. "I would be ashamed if everyone knew that I was married to a girl who had experience; but deep down, I do not care less."

Mayar caught my attention with her long blonde hair, made up face, and perfect figure that showed clearly through her tight-fitting low waist jeans and body-hugging shirt. She was sitting alone when I approached her, introduced myself, and asked permission to join her. I did not need to ask many questions; she did all the talking on her own. "I am 27 and, as you can see, I am very pretty. I date a lot and my rules change depending on the person I am going out with; if he is '**efl**' – narrow-minded – I will dress up less provocatively and will just let him pick up the check. If he is one of those fake modern guys who wear cargo pants to hide their galabeyas, I beat him at his game too by showing everything that he cannot touch. I am never myself with Egyptian men; I feel that I am always seen through a microscope and my slightest expression of my feelings will be used against me. When I am with a foreigner, I am more expressive. I am not a slut as people call me."

Surprisingly enough, none of the people I talked to said that they did something or withheld from doing something because they wanted to; it was never their innate choice, it was always a reaction to 'people'; those 'people', along with ghosts, demons, and spirits, are in the same category in my head - they are there but we have our separate lives and our paths don't cross. I don't fetch them and they don't come after me - end of story.

***

Wrapped up in her beautiful Indian Sari, Maya looked at the Kama Sutra teacher and asked about the difference between shame and honor as tears rolled down her cheeks. The experienced courtesan looked back at her, smiled, and told her that shame and honor are the two faces of the same coin. With Maya's ears I listened to the story of a king who had to go to war; on the night of the king's departure, his wife washed his feet in a water basin. With this water, she washed her face every day the king was at war. The night the king returned he went directly to Rasa, the courtesan. The queen was humiliated in the name of honor, the courtesan was honored in the name of shame, Maya was hurt in the name of revenge, and I am lost in the name of love!

Because of my tendency to be self-sufficient and independent, my best friend once told me that I am the ideal material for a mistress or a second wife. I laughed at her ten years ago but today, her words came back to me as I threw myself into the heart of an affair, and I am now wallowing in shame. In an attempt to sort out my personal mess, I found out that "Shame is a reaction to other people's criticism, an acute personal chagrin at our failure to live up to our obligations and the expectations others have of us. Personal desires are sunk in the collective expectation. (Shame is) the primary device for gaining control over children and maintaining control over adults," wrote Paul G. Hiebert in his Anthropological Insights for Missionaries.

Apart from social expectations and cultural norms, there was nothing deep down in the core of my character to stop me from being with a man who had someone else – a girlfriend not a wife! As long as we were kept in separate lanes and led separate lives, a self delusional version of me did not see a problem with a man who has two girlfriends. I knew that I was possessive and that I hated sharing but I hushed the competitive female instinct with promises that I would win. As a Taekwondo player, I was taught how to defend my property, both mentally and physically. The fighter in me fantasized about the knockout that would kick her non-Egyptian face out of the combat arena. The spirit of a vicious tigress possessed me and, in my head, I tore my rival to pieces with my fangs and claws.

Away from right and wrong, I enjoyed being the one he longed to be with; I was the desired fantasy and she was the plain reality; she was what pushed him away and I was what pulled him closer; I lured him with fiction and she trapped him in facts; with me he flew and in her world he crashed; my world was colored in shades of pink and scented with aromas from the orient, while her world was made of sharp lines and clear-cut details. I entertained him with my endless stories, my well defined aliases flew him from one cloud to the other, and I felt him aching for me. I loved being a fantasy until reality hit me in the face.

Reality felt jealous, tasted bitter, looked ugly, smelled rotten, and sounded like the screeching of chalk on a board. Paralyzed for a moment with a sharp yet brief pain, I faced him with one long gaze and decided to end my flight. I pushed one pause button after the other until I no longer felt his presence. I was in my cockpit alone looking at a distant runway. There was no air traffic controller at the other end of my pilot's headset; I was on my own in the mess that I had dragged myself into. I feared steering my plane into another unrecoverable nosedive. I did not want another crash. As my heartbeats and the pace of my thoughts slowed down, I put my wheels down, lined up my plane, and kept my wings straight. I smoothly touched down and my brakes kicked in automatically as I hit solid ground.

As I got off the plane, I felt like a hero that had saved many lives from a horrible, inevitable crash; no casualties, no injuries, and little loss to remember. I sighed as I was welcomed back on earth by many of my friends who told me that in our age we are only left with five options when it comes to men: married and hunting, divorced and messed up, widowed and mourning, single and traumatized, or single and much younger. I am the master of the options game and I just do not like the menu of men they are offering me. I also did not like my short-haul flight. I felt like a smuggled bag of worthless scrap that could be dumped at the sight of the farthest raid.

Moral of the story: do as you would be done by, all who live must surely die, and all who meet will surely part, what goes around comes around, he who diggeth a pit shall fall therein, and he that rolleth a stone, it will return upon him. I was like a monkey trying to snatch the moon's reflection on the water; I risked drowning, did not reach the moon, and paved the way to frustration. I ridded myself of the shackles of shame that weighed on my consciousness as I reminded myself that I was not created to meet expectations of others. Shame and guilt are socially inflicted negative feelings. This is the price tag of growing up; this is the definition of experience. I smiled as the details of my flight crossed my mind and I made up my mind – next time, I will be a fantasy with no reality to compete with.

***

It was St. Valentine's Day in 2000 when I first heard Losing my Religion. I was happily dancing to the beat until the lyrics hit me. My feet lost the rhythm and I came to a complete stop. How could anyone sing along, or dance to, such a song; "That's me in the corner … That's me in the spotlight … Losing my religion … Trying to keep up with you … I thought that I heard you laughing … I thought that I heard you sing … I think I thought I saw you try." It was the first of many more things to challenge my deeply rooted conviction that religion is neither open for questioning nor subject to doubt. I was brought up, like many other Egyptians, to take religion for granted. Asking "why?" is transgression and wondering is the first step of atheism.

Last month, my aunt invited me, along with all my siblings, for dinner to welcome our American-born cousin and his wife who were in town. I was happy to meet up with my cousin. There was a time when we talked about everything from cultural differences and social pretences to physics and astronomy. Seven years ago Ahmed got very religious, but he was still fun to be around; his soul and essence were untouched. Two years ago he got married to the daughter of a sheikh. I met her briefly after the wedding; I only saw her eyes. That night we did not shake hands, let alone talk. His wife launched an attack on me for taking off the veil ten years ago, saying that I looked prettier before and that I had the light of God on my face instead of make-up! When we all took our seats at the big dining table, Ahmed's wife sat alone in the living room. Our kind hostess left her food and joined her.

One thought haunted my drive home: this utter humiliation cannot come from God. God loves us! He did not create us to doubt us! He has faith in us just as much as we have faith in Him! He does not think of us as pieces of meat governed by lust! Instead of going to bed, I went on a treasure hunt; I was looking for material on the relationship between men and women. On IslamToday.com,

Sheikh Sami Al Majid had compiled all the verses and quotes I needed. I loved his opening statement; kind of defies the purpose! "We cannot find direct references in the Qur'ân and Sunnah that say that free mixing between men and women is unlawful." The sheikh continued, saying that Islam "has defined the limits of interaction between men and women. Moreover, Islam has closed all doors that lead to temptation and promiscuity."

He quoted scholars saying that a judge should try women separately from men, women are not obligated to attend the Friday prayers, a party invitation may be refused if there will be any clear wrongdoing at the party because "under these circumstances, desires are kindled and temptations are greater, and regrettable things happen, as is seen time and again in co-ed schools and mixed social events," said the sheikh as he listed the evidence:

1. Allah says: *"And when you ask the ladies for anything, ask them from before a screen. That makes for greater purity for your hearts and for theirs."* [Sûrah al-Ahzâb: 53]

2. The Prophet said: *"Never is a man alone with a woman except that Satan is the third party with them.*

3. The Prophet also said: *"Do not enter into the company of women."* A man then asked him: "What about her male in-laws?" The Prophet replied: *"The in-law is the most dangerous."*

4. The Prophet also said: *"It is better for one of you to be pierced by a steel pin in his head than to touch the hand of a strange woman."*

5. The Qur'an clearly forbids women from being soft of speech while talking to men. Allah says: *"Be not too complaisant of speech, lest one in whose heart is a disease should be moved with desire: but speak with a speech (that is) proper."* [Sûrah al-Ahzâb: 32]

6. The Prophet said: *"Any woman who puts on perfume then goes and passes by some men to let them find her scent is a type of adulteress."*

7. Allah says: *"Nor come nigh to adultery."* In this verse, Allah does not say "Do not commit adultery" but tells us not even to come close to it.

8. Allah says: *"Say to the believing men that they should lower their gaze and guard their modesty: that will make for greater purity for them."* And says: *"And say to the believing women that they should lower their gaze and guard their modesty."*[Sûrah al-Nûr:30-31]

This shows us how men and women are to conduct themselves.

As if that was not enough research for me, I had to take my confusion into the chat room; I told Sherif that the devil was in our heads and that temptation came from within. He was shocked, and asked me if I am a believer. I told him that I am a believer in a great God and in a merciful religion, but people who came between us and God's book did all the damage; I was not talking about prophets, I was talking about sheikhs who try to interpret God. He told me that the Qur'an mentioned the devil clearly. I told him that the Qur'an also mentioned Heaven and Hell clearly, but the words and visuals used were metaphorical; a palace is not a palace, a river is not a river, and a devil is not a devil. I asked Sherif to try to let go of the interpretations that we were fed growing up, but he insisted that Satan was an outside force; he is the source of temptation. I asked him about the holy month of Ramadan; God promised us that the demons would be chained, so where did temptation come from? At this point I mentally signed out.

From Sherif I moved to Ehab. I told him that I was writing an article about questioning religion. He told me that this was a place where angels feared to tread. I shared with him a link to an article entitled Wondrous Treatment of Women in Islam. He said that it must have been written by some "ignorant worm". He declared his dislike of the article from the start. I asked him to leave the tone of the article aside and to focus on the facts. He refused, saying: "I am one of those people who believe that our religion is without reproach ... if we choose to go astray here or there then we do it at our own peril... we should not try and fault our religion to find excuse for our own behaviors. I am no saint but I know where not to cross the line ... no matter how much of a drone I may seem to be, there is no heroism in challenging God." I asked him if he believed that if a man and a woman were left unattended to, the third party would be the devil. He jokingly said that he did; not because he knew the devil but because he knew guys.

My chat with Ehab ended when he said that in the absence of light, dark prevails, referring to me, I guess. I replied by telling him that one man's poison is another man's bread; it is all a matter of perception. In this case light and dark are very relative and are subject to our interpretations. Islam promotes the principles of trust, integrity, honesty, wisdom, and freedom of choice. Why did this sheikh, and others, turn a loving forgiving God into a tyrant? Why did they interpret the verses to favor one gender over the other, when God created us as equal? Darkness is in the head of someone who says that for women to go about uncovered in the company of men is inarguably a gross violation of God's commands. It is pitch black in a world that believes that everything that may seduce a person to fall into adultery is unlawful. Depraved of light are those who fear getting turned on by shaking hands with a woman or by smelling her perfume. Blind are those who lock their God-given brains in their stubborn skulls, and let others think on their behalf!

***

"The End justifies the Means" is quoted in our everyday life from Niccolo Machiavelli's book, The Prince. So, if the end is getting a ring on your naked left-hand finger, then any lie you throw in the way of Prince Charming is an acceptable means to a justifiable end. What does he want to hear? That you are a virgin? That you have never been kissed? That you have never been in love? That you have never dated? That he is the first and will certainly be the last? That you are a God-sent angel from heaven? Instead of a happily-ever-after ending to your story, the truth will just bring it to a sudden, humiliating ending; hence, manoeuvring is called for to perfect this Machiavellian plan.

So let's assume that we have a girl who is poor beyond poverty, more ambitious than Lady Macbeth, is paying her tuition fees, and is saving for her dowry. This girl chose the least trodden path as a means to her end; she began selling her body bit by bit for the highest bidders, yet holding on to her virginity; kissing has a price, exploring adds to the bill, and making out is rated differently. Advanced services like hand jobs, fellatio (oral sex), and backdoor sex fall in another category. Those girls and their activities shed a florescent light on the definition of prostitution.

"Where there is a will, there is a way," my mom used to remind me whenever my determination failed me, and those girls were willing to prostitute themselves, they just needed to find a way to do so while preserving their virginity. I was first triggered to write this piece on backdoor sex when I read that some girls went to the attorney general and filed a complaint against Hala Sarhan for paying them off and coaching them into pretending to be prostitutes on her show. They said that she promised that their identities would be hidden, but when the show was aired they were scandalized because everyone who knew them could recognize them. The girls were presented to forensics so they could prove that they were not prostitutes, as Hala's show claimed. The forensic report concluded that they were all virgins with intact hymens, however they showed signs of heavy anal use; the signs included abrasions on the anal opening and a 'funneled' anus.

Later on, I received an email with a scan of an article from Al Fagr newspaper by Amira Melsh that had a shocking headline: 80% of Prostitutes are Virgins then another article followed by Wael Abdel Fattah, entitled Virgin Prostitution in Egypt. Both articles researched the entangled webs of vice, pimps, strategies and schemes to lure new girls, rules for dealing with customers, pricing strategies, and guarantees. The girls themselves were discussed, revealing their ages and motives; the girls made it very clear to the 'customer' that they were to remain virgins. In the investigation, they said that most of their customers were Arabs who paid a lot for backdoor sex, many young Egyptians who only wanted to be touched and relieved, and 50-plus men who wanted to feel young again.

Some of the girls had what sounded like strategic goals for a five-year plan before they retired, put it all behind them, and got married to their cuckolded Prince Charming who would flaunt his manhood along with the virginity of his bride. The plan entailed goals such as buying a car, a down payment for a house, and some cash to start their own business. "What is better to fill the gap between aspirations and reality, than a girl's body?" said 25-year-old Nagwan, who is a virgin herself and runs a well structured web; someone is in charge of setting up the house, while another is in charge of bringing in the customers; recruiting new girls is a very segmented process that covers school girls, college girls, married women, and mothers. "Our customers have different needs and tastes and it is our job to please the customer," concluded Nagwan.

"I come from a poor family in Sharkia," said Sara "and I have big dreams of living comfortably and of getting married and having kids of my own. I have an image and a reputation to maintain in this society, this is why most of my business meetings are held in Zamalek and Mohandeseen with Arabs; no one will know me and I will never see them again. They are also more generous and more accepting of my sole condition – I have to remain a virgin," said Sara in her interview.

As usual, I ran to my laptop and logged on to an Arabic language dating site where I pretended to be a Kuwaiti guy coming on vacation to Egypt and looking for an escort. I did not approach anyone; I just posted a photo and waited. I did not wait long before my inbox was filled with messages from girls of different ages typing, in Arabic, their needs and requests. I picked one girl who specified backdoor sex as the ultimate form of intercourse and she clearly stated that she was a virgin and that she wanted to stay so.

I tried to bargain for full intercourse but she was adamant; I learnt that she came from a conservative family and that she wanted a better life. "If I get married to someone from that level I will remain poor but if I am rich, I can marry rich," she explained. Her services covered airport pick up, arranging for a rented car, outings, kissing and the like, hand jobs and the like, backdoor sex, and sleeping over. She was very forward about her demands and shrewd in negotiating each item. The deal went sour when I insisted on full intercourse.

In the old days, prostitutes had distinctive features: the way they laughed, talked, walked, dressed, wore make-up, and chewed gum. Nowadays, they could be anyone you meet in a shop, supermarket, college, or outing. When our society placed all the emphasis on the presence or absence of a piece of meat, a new breed of Machiavellian call girls was born. They used society's best argument to their favor; socially speaking, honor is linked to the presence of a hymen, and they will have a hymen to show on their wedding night. Innocence, integrity, and the truth sunk deep down in our social gutters and now we have to live in the stink of lies and the stench of corruption. They learned that our laws turn the customer into a witness and that the only proof of their innocence is virginity. They found out that where there is a will, there is a way; and when the front door is locked, open the back door!

***

Like a sword, the S word cuts through our lives; starting and ending relationships; labeling and tagging people; torturing some and relieving others. I grew up watching our Egyptian cinema turning sex into a shameful, repulsive act where the woman is defeated and the man is delighted. The message was very clear: women who 'give in' to men without a legally binding document end up suffering one way or the other. The S word turns them into social outcasts, black sheep, or infamous, notorious creatures of the night. The man usually vanishes, leaving behind a bereaved creature pulling her hair and tearing apart what's left of her clothes as a sign of intense remorse. Some of those women were portrayed to show further suffering when the seed of the affair blossoms into a child. With nothing but disdain and a curled lip, the voice of our intact society would echo in our ears saying, "You've been warned!"

In our modern cinema, girls can flirt and tease as much as they please, but the S word is still frowned upon. Those engaging in premarital sex strive throughout the movie to set two wrongs right – and of course it is the girl who is always doing her very best to get a ring on the damn finger. Other tragic heroines, whose character flaw is their lustful nature, have to go through a painful catharsis whereby they are humiliated, rejected, mortified, and eventually forgiven, or killed in an accident. In the first denouement, being forgiven in this sense means that they have learnt their lesson and that they will lead a life of penance and 'virtue' until a fine gentleman sees how far they have changed and kindly accepts to give them a ring. In the second scenario - where they die - they have paid in full for their mortal sin and now they can just die to set an example for the living.

Today a fellow writer, in a casual chat, asked me why girls refuse and adamantly resist getting intimate with their beau. He complained of the fact that girls feel that the S word impacts the interest, or the lack of interest, of a guy in a girl. He bluntly asked me why girls fear losing the guy once they have sex with him. I was not the only one watching those movies; I could even consider myself lucky because I was a late bloomer in my relationship with the silver screen. Decade after another, such movies spread the guilt-based culture in our shame-based society. As if FGM (female genital mutilation) was not enough to create lifetime barriers between our girls and their sexuality, we have a whole culture preaching the virtue of a hymen.

Arabic movies, books, and anecdotes planted a deeply rooted conviction that girls who are 'dishonorable' are not fit for being wives or mothers. The same influences caused men to believe that a girl who expresses her love physically is loose; hence the famous analogies between a girl's honor and a match stick, a brand new car and a secondhand car, and the famous piece of meat covered in sticky flies. My maid once noticed that my cats were not playing together and threw me a casual comment, saying, "Why would he want to even see her face … he already took what he wanted … he is just a man!"

I have many male friends who, in my presence, share their success stories and conquests in the female world. Their verbiage and jargon are of the most offensive type; verbs like jumped, humped, and scored are very popular. Once the girl loses touch with the ground, she falls … she falls hard and is most likely to break her neck, smash her head, or crack her back. She survives the fall only to live with a permanent disability. Experience has taught girls to hold back; they have learnt to disguise their feelings in a cloak of callousness for self-preservation purposes. Our generation of men and women are confused; everything that they were taught as kids is being questioned as adults. Our very same inhibited women and our very own conservative men, once in the presence of a foreigner, are transformed. The women no longer feel judged and the men no longer feel pressured and questioned – what a mess!

I am not for or anti premarital sex. There are so many variables in the equation and our society is not ready for a generalization of any sort at this point of time; if I tell girls to go ahead and to release their inhibitions, I will be damned. If I tell them to resist and to fight the natural urge for intimacy, I am a lying hypocrite. I will just leave it at the point where it is a case-by-case scenario and I will conclude on a final note to the guys: mental shackles are way worse than metal shackles. We will get out of our dungeons when we no longer fear your dragons.

***

"I met someone," she said in a voice that lacked the buzz of a new relationship.

"But?" I asked, knowing that there had to be a "but".

"He is 8 years younger!"

I understand why a woman my age, or older, could be attracted to someone who is younger, or much younger; yet, I failed to grasp the logic – if such a word exists – behind young men who willingly, consensually, freely choose to dive into a relationship with someone who is ten years older than he is. By a relationship I do not mean an affair, I am referring to a fully fledged relationship that incorporates all the rules of Victorian courtship – the wining and dining, the meet my friends and meet your friends, the call me and call you, and the love you and miss you routines.

I am secretly growing more insecure in the presence of younger girls, but obviously I have competitive advantages that I am not aware of. I am no exception to this new perplexing rule; A, N, M, and H are four of my friends whose ages range from 37 to 47, and they are attracting guys who are at best 8 years younger. My last four attempts at dating were with guys whose ages ranged from 23 to 28. My Facebook account is bombarded with friend requests from a breed that is a decade younger than I am. My blog is piling up comments from angry bloggers who recently developed facial hair. Something is wrong!! How do we, older women, attract them - younger guys?

I am bad at guessing! I had to ask them! I needed to hack their little green brains and find out the answer. My classroom – there is no better place to start. Instead of a pop quiz in marketing, I handed them a piece of paper with one question and I gave them an hour to give me the answer that has been confusing the heck out of me. The question was: If you had a choice, would you rather date someone your age or, would you date me, or someone else, knowing that there is more or less ten years of difference in age? Why yes? Why no? The look on their faces was priceless! The silence that filled the room was louder than anything they would have said. They were looking at me for clarification and I gave them none. I told them that the clock was ticking and that I was serious.

In an hour the answer sheets were on my desk and I impatiently began checking their responses. There were some flattering comments about my eyes and smile and there were some semi-insulting comments about my temper and insanity. As I went deeper into their explanations, my eyes grew wider in shock as I found out the major points of differentiation that make those guys favor ripe apples – as one student put it down. A combined list would say that we are more mature, independent, experienced, understanding, and appreciative of the little things young girls take for granted. We have careers and are busy with important and meaningful stuff. We are good listeners and we give good advice. The list goes on to highlight our graces: secure, intellectual, connected, and confident.

One student said that we do not ask silly questions and we do not get upset over stupid things like, "Do you love me? Do I look good? Why didn't you call? Where were you? Who's that girl? Or I have a curfew, I cannot be seen with you, and let's cruise." Some guys said that being with an older woman would make younger women interested. "If I were to date you, young girls would be jealous and they would want to know what is so special about me that would make an icon like you go out with me. I must be really mature and experienced to satisfy you." Another student was very honest when he said, "You will pick up the check all the time; this is the price you will pay for going out with a hot dude like myself – I mean you know I am young and I cannot afford your outings." Several opinions shed light on expectations: "Girls my age want to get married – not to me in particular, they just want to get married. You will not rush me into meeting your family and will not bother me with questions about the future. Older women are down to earth and they just want to live the moment."

On the more aggressive side, a guy replied saying that "I like to think of it as a charitable act of goodwill. If being around someone who is going downhill would make her feel better, then so be it. I also enjoy how her younger female friends look at me. Some of them even flirt." Another guy said that "behind their confident, experienced façade, older women need to be held and touched. They need a sharp pencil – if you know what I mean (wink)." Outside the classroom, a blogger told me, face to face, that older women are just a phase "I am learning and gaining experience so I will be ready for a girl my age. Being with her makes me feel so grown up but there will be a time when I go back in the time machine to my real age. It is never serious. There is an implicit deal between me and my girlfriend, if you want to call her so, that there is no happily ever after end to our relationship."

I was visiting 37-year-old divorced N a few months ago at her place and we were having the usual girl talks until she told me that her boyfriend was coming. I wanted to leave but she insisted that I meett him. I asked her what he did for a living and she told me that he was an account executive in an agency. I then asked her how they met and she said that they had met online. I asked her if he was married; she laughed, and told me that he was 28. I knew that she was lonely and that her dating options were next to disgusting, and I could understand her reasons for dating a younger guy, but I was super curious about his reasons, especially when I saw him. He was well groomed, well spoken, well dressed, and well bred. I was too shy to ask him about his interest in my friend, so I waited till he was gone and I asked her to give me her best guess for his motives.

She told me that he was fascinated by her day-to-day stories – the same stories that bored men her age. When it came to his personal or professional life, he found her advice indispensable. Plus of course the fact that she had her own place, lived alone, and was in touch with her feminine side. She told me that she offered him the comfort, space, and freedom that young girls could not provide. N would never ask him any question that started with why, when, who, where, how, what, how long, or how often. She is independent – mentally and emotionally – and with his monthly 3,000 Egyptian Pounds, it is not likely that he could be entertaining any ideas of getting married soon. N was very comfortable analyzing his motives. It did not cross my mind to ask Santa for a man my age or a few years older; I thought it went without saying that younger guys were not an option. I used to wonder what some of my friends found in a guy who was 5, 7, or 10 years younger than they were.

I used to wonder what a young guy had to say to someone who was carrying her schoolbag when he was sucking on his thumb, and was under no illusion that this could be love or that it could end up with something old, something new, or something borrowed and something blue.

A 28-year-old guy was wooing me, and after I declared my age, he said with a huge smile on his face that women are like apples: the older they grow the riper they become. Sarcastic as usual, I said that ripe apples are bruised from the inside and have visible brown patches. I was a bit self conscious when I added that this was a sign that they were approaching their expiry date. My smart cookie said that those brown patches are sweeter, softer, more tender, and much tastier than the rest of the apple. I could not keep up with the witty conversation. I did like the puppy look in his eyes. I was falling, and, ironically speaking, I resorted to the Irish proverb that says: *When the apple is ripe it will fall!*

***

My heart went out to those ladies who had to bear the inquisitive eyes that followed them wherever they took their toy boy. I was so certain that I would never walk the famous mile in their shoes. I assured myself that I was bulletproof safe from that kind of disgusting despair. I knew that I would never be as lonely or as insane as they were. I surprised myself ... I was wrong!

It all started when I noticed that 22 and 23-year-old guys found me attractive; whether they were students in my classes or trainees in my workshops, I used to smile and gently push them out of my way. I felt flattered, but I was always in control of my actions and emotions. Last year I made a slight exception – a year or two younger is not such a big deal, especially if he is well travelled, well exposed, and well set in his career. My toy-boy alarm was in the making; just the thought of me settling for this type of public humiliation gave me immediate palpitations.

Last January, a 24-year-old writer developed a crush on me; he was young, cute, and, on top of it all, he had great brains. Instead of redirecting his route away from me, I caught myself red-handed flirting with him. A dreamy, "I don't want to lose you" flew out of his mouth to slap me on the face. The harsh wake-up call startled me ... what on earth was I doing? But then I ignored the voice of reason and enjoyed listening to his passionate compliments about how I made him feel and how much he wanted to be with me. He got attached and I sobered up; I vanished and he was hurt.

A few weeks later, I crossed paths with another writer – 7 years younger! This time my defenses were up and I would not allow myself to repeat my previous mistake. I turned this connection into an online intellectual friendship but I am still curious about the other side of the fence. I dedicated a special dark corner in my head where I buried all such thoughts and feelings – they just scared me. I am in my 30s but luckily, because I tend to be well maintained, I do not look it – it was never about looks, was it?

I am a single, independent career-oriented girl who is starved for love and attention. I miss being in a relationship and I miss the little things that add a warming flavor to my spreadsheet of a life: the surprises, the love words, the excitement before a date, the dreamy reminiscence after a date, and the phone calls that are directly wired to my heart. I want to have a plan for the weekend and someone to look forward to talking to. I want to come out of my class to find a missed call or a text message from someone – not my mother, not my friends, and not work-related.

Is it that I do not meet enough men? Is it that I do not attract them? No! There are plenty of them around me but I just do not like them. I do not like their baggage; be it an ex wife, a current wife, kids, bad experiences, imbedded resentment for women, commitment phobia, independence-related selfishness, emotional stinginess, financial stinginess, lack of expressiveness, over-eagerness, hair loss, muscle loss, a spare tire around their waist, or a midlife crisis. Men who are my age, or a bit older, have given up on life or given in to life.

They are either married, defeated, depressive, deformed, or plain ugly. The few who are eligible candidates do not want to be with me, my dozen professions, and my radical opinions. They do not want an equal and cannot accept a superior; they want a young girl who they can control, boss around, guide, and manipulate in the name of love! They want a young mother for their kids and an inexperienced wife in their bed. Let's face it: at the age of 35, a guy can easily have a healthy relationship with someone who is 25, 26, 27, or 28 years old. I am developing a scary form of cannibalism; young hearts, fresh skin, and green minds attract me. I love the puppy-love look in their hope-filled eyes, the sweet compliments, the need to be with me and around me, the attention, the eagerness to please, the fear of losing me, and the pride of showing me off to their friends.

The sad news is that just as much as I can see through the lonely, over-eager older guys, younger guys can see through the false, tough façade that I so brilliantly set up for myself. I have become so trained on picking up the vibes of desperate hunters, and young guys can easily sense my cannibalism and need for affection. I have no living proof of the success or the continuity of any such toy boy relationships. I do not like the way I see the future – I see a 45-year-old hag hunting young mouthwatering kids and devouring their hopes, aspirations, and futures. This is topping the chart of my worst fears. I am so vulnerable; I have nightmares – toy boy nightmares.

***

"You are running out of time!" typed a long-lost, recently-found schoolmate from childhood upon knowing that I was not married yet. I wanted to flaunt my long list of achievements but she kept ticking and tocking. I told her I have a great career in public relations, she was not interested; I said I am sharing my working experience with my students, she said they were not my kids; I explained how companies use me to enhance the skills of their employees, she wondered why I did not want children; I sent her my blogs to read everything I have ever written and published, she said she would read them when her kids were sleeping; I told her I am doing a TV show on relationships, she ordered me to get real! She sounded so content being married with two kids; I did not sense genuine happiness in her tone though. As if she had only come online to disturb my peace, she wished me luck and left the chat. Once again I felt like the little girl I once was, trying to show off my handmade Kleenex flowers when no one was really interested!

The world seemed to be conspiring against me when I got a call from my mom a few minutes later. After the usual hellos, in her adorable enthusiastic tone, my mom shared with me a brilliant idea: I am to find a man with good genes, get married, get pregnant, and get divorced right away. I laughed my heart out. I wished I could hug her. She thought I was mocking her with my laughter and she was ever so intent on making her point. She flashed the biological clock pepper spray in my face as she quoted a doctor on TV: "As women age, the quality and quantity of their eggs decline, thus affecting fertilization success, embryo quality, and pregnancy rate. The rate of decline varies from one woman the other, but overall, fertility begins to decline slowly in a woman's 30s, with the greatest decline happening after the age of 35." I was no longer laughing as I felt trapped between a huge rugged rock and a very hard place; part of me acknowledged what my mom said, yet another part insisted on doing it the right way. I want a child with the right man; I had never wanted any of the men who had come my way to be the father of any baby I gave birth to.

The other day I joined a group of friends, and their friends, for lunch in the town's hottest Italian restaurant. My best friend literally begged me to keep my views to myself and asked me not to turn the outing into a futile debate. I was a bit insulted, but I gave her my promise. Finding my cute resemblance in my squeaky wooden chair, I sat, smiled, nodded, and managed a giggle when needed. I was about to dive into my bowl of soup, when one of the single guys at the table proudly stated that men were privileged with their ability to 'impregnate' a woman regardless of their age. Thinking of my friend, instead of jumping at his throat, I decided to see what the other guys and girls on the table had to say. The married women used the word 'compromise' many times – especially when looking towards their husbands. The married men used the word 'favor' at lot - especially when looking towards their wives. The single girls were drowning in helplessness, the single guys were choking on their private jokes, and my friend was pressing my hand when she should have gagged my mouth.

I threw the first dart at the guy who was bragging about his ability to have kids at any age as I faced him with the sad truth: yes, he could have a kid at the age of 45 but he will never give him the fun that a 25-year-old young dad can give him. He will feel old, look old, act old, and be old. The second dart targeted married men: I asked each of the wives to make a wish – five traits that they would like to be passed on from their husband to their son or daughter. After the initial humming, came a silence, some gap fillers, and then a few incoherent words that just reflected how these women are not convinced of the men they chose. The men looked offended, but that was no excuse for me to spare them; it was their turn to tell me the five qualities that they wished the wives had said. Their masculine faces looked dignified and proud as they waved the flags of responsibility, generosity, sensibility, and the like. I watched as the male and female eyes met; the men threatened and the women recoiled. The men looked victorious, the women looked revolted, and I could not touch my soup.

The single 33, 34, 36, and 40-year-old girls began telling their tales of rejection that basically rotated on the fact that he, or his mother, thought they were too old to have kids. They talked about the inquisitive eyes, questioning looks, the muttering, the murmuring, the whispering, and the curled lips that stalk them in weddings, parties, gatherings, and outings. Society and family deny them the right to choose and to refuse because they are 'too old'. They struggle with their self-esteem and self-fulfillment, and are torn apart between their hormones, nesting phases, and settling down urges - we ladies suffer! I barged in again, lending my fellow single females a supporting hand. I played my favorite Libra game: single and happy, or married and miserable? Single gal or single mom? No man or wrong man? No kids or wrong kids? I hit a bull's eye when I mentioned the possibility of adoption; if your maternal instinct is nagging non-stop and Mr. Right took a wrong turn on his way to you, nonetheless, you can still be a mother. Options start from nephews and nieces, cats and dogs, to sponsored orphans and live-in orphans. Motherhood is not about getting pregnant and giving birth; motherhood is all about nurturing and caring – be it a warm hug, sound advice, a shoulder to cry on, or a comforting smile. Having spoken my mind, the single girls were silent and pensive, and the single guys were silent and attentive – I rested my case and my soup was cold.

***

Between the excitement of a new job and the weight of its big responsibilities, I found the time to meet up with my friend D one evening right after work. We were both run down but we were longing for the tête-a-tête girly chat. I seated myself in front of her, laid my exhausted body on the chair, and ordered all the comfort food on the menu. From the work round-up to the social gossip, we jumped from one topic to the other, laughing and giggling like school girls at a slumber party. We suddenly stopped talking when the couple at the adjacent table received their check.

The girl looked from the check to the ceiling and seemed to trace an invisible fly. Her partner looked at the check, hesitantly put his hand in his pocket, took two or three 10-pound bills, put them on the tray, and then pushed the tray – with the check – towards the girl with a cough – and probably a kick in her leg. The girl let go of her imaginary friend, looked at the check, curled her lower lip, threw a few more bills on the tray, and stood up. There was no eye-contact between them as she took her purse and sped towards the door – the guy was two steps behind. D and I looked at one another and laughed.

"Do you think they will last?" I asked her innocently.

"He is half a man." D replied with a solemn face.

"He did not do anything wrong" I said, "Sharing the bill is perfectly normal. They both seem young and most probably he could not afford it."

D totally disagreed with me; she told me that she would never respect a man who would let her pick up the check, or half of the check. D believed that if a man were to take a girl out on a date, or an outing, he has to be a man about it. "It is an honor for him to have the pleasure of her company and a real man would never let a girl pay a penny – especially if they were more than casual friends." I was not sure what to think ... I had never given that particular issue any thought. I have always felt obliged to reach out for my purse, even if the man said he would pay. Now that I am thinking about it, I tend to believe that somewhere deep down, I feel that if I did not share the bill, I have somehow betrayed myself as though I am allowing him to buy part of me, not my dinner or lunch. D's perspective runs deeper than that.

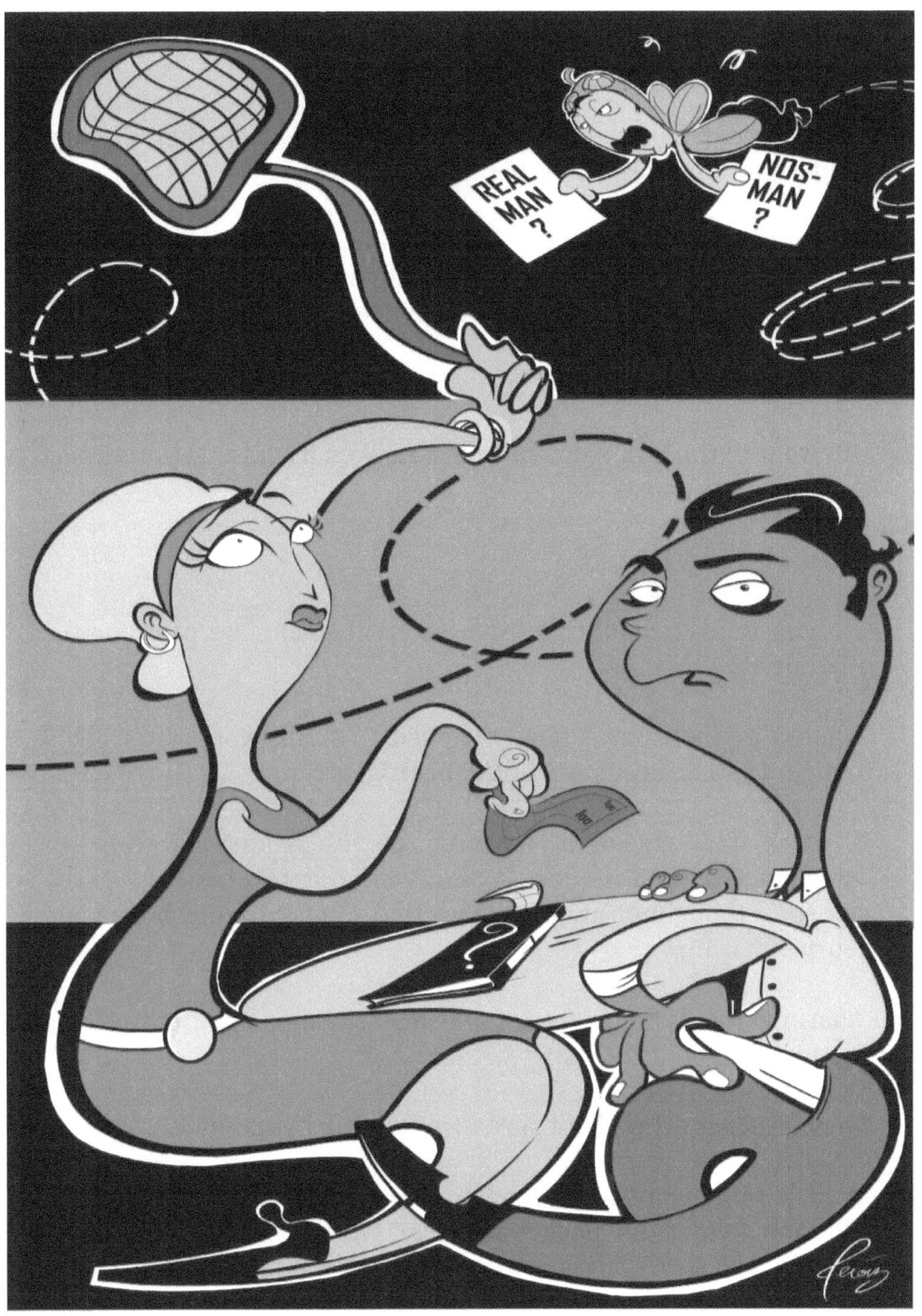

"A man should be responsible, and a responsible man takes total and utter care of the needs of his woman."

I interrupted D, asking, "Do those needs include her clothes, makeup, accessories, and other luxuries?"

"Yes of course!" D corrected me. "Let's assume that I am married to a man, and we decided to travel, do you think I will pay for my ticket, accommodation, and food?"

I had no reply – I had never really thought about it.

"If I want to throw a party for our family or friends, do you expect me to share the cost?"

Again, I had a blank face.

"Do you think I should pay the electricity bill if he pays for the other utilities?"

"I guess it is normal" I finally replied. "You do work, after all." I thought I had an argument until I heard her reply.

"I work for my own reasons, be it self-actualization or entertainment, and no decent man will accept to take any of my money." I thought of my mom, and said, "But it is your house and you are sharing."

"Sharing? This is not fair! I am sharing his responsibilities but is he sharing mine?"

"In what sense?" I was not sure I was getting her point.

"A man should bring the money, put food on the table, pay the bills, and give me my pocket money. A woman, on the other hand, should make sure the money is well spent, the food on the table is cooked, the house is clean, the kids are brought up well, and the man is comfortable and taken care of. By sharing my salary, I am taking part of his load off his shoulders. Will he share my load too, or will he still expect to be served and obeyed?"

She saw my perplexed face and continued, saying, "Most men nowadays want the woman to share his burdens along with her initial responsibility. If this was a company, and they were equal shareholders, using my logic, his share would be 25%. Now why would I want a man who is in this lifetime partnership with 25%? Why would I want to be with half a man?"

I resorted to the stuttering economy and the expensive cost of living, saying, "Very few men now can take full care of the financial responsibilities. You might never get married D."

"Let's assume once again that I did not meet my Mr. Real Man, and let's assume that I grew to like one of the current 'half men', then his shares in this partnership do not grant him neither a superior word nor an upper hand. It is only fair and natural that if he is half a man, he deserves half a woman."
I had one last question for D: "If you were to get married to a 'real man' as per your classification, would you fully give in to his wishes and commands?"

"Give me examples," D exclaimed.

"If he does not want you to go out, or if he does not like an outfit, a friend, or anything you want to do, will you do as he says?" I seemed to gasp for air just thinking of the possibility of a man holding my reign.

"Yes … I will … He earned it and I owe it to him," D concluded.

Ok then, I am half a woman ... I want to have a higher vote ... I do not want to owe this kind of obedience to a man ... and please ... please do not start the religion argument with me!

***

Dear Narcissistic Jerk,

Please do not take this letter personally; I neither mean insult nor injury. I am writing to you on behalf of all the females that I know, and those that I do not know. Who? You know who; the doormats. Oh please, do not give me that face!

To be more specific, I am representing the women who stay in relationships with worthless men like your kind self; women who have no demands; who give without expectations; whose return on investment is your humble smirk. Yes, the ones who can do much better but because of some fatal flaw with their self-perception, they settle for half the man they deserve. Oops! Did that hurt?

Hold your horses! I am not done yet! I have not even started! Let me remind you of the long list of your offences: falsifying a male ID on the grounds of facial hair and protrusions, theft of their hearts, deception to gain access to their lives, evading liability relating to any of your actions, trespassing to other feminine pastures, assault of their friends, battery of their ego, unlawful wounding of their self-esteem, wounding with intent of their pride, reck-lessness throughout the relationship, negligence of their needs, intimidation and threats, conspiracy against their peace of mind, and murder of their happily-ever-after dreams.

If I were to sentence you to prison for all your crimes, I would sentence you to an eternity of loneliness and suffering. I would have you stoned for every tear a woman shed for you. I would have you whipped for every dagger-of-a-word you threw in her heart. Like a plucked chicken, I would toss you in boiling water for every jealous moment you caused her. I would stick an iron rod in each ear that would not listen to her desperate pleas. They should be broken, those fingers that hurt when they promised to heal. Should have been cut …. I will let you figure that one out on your own!

She wanted you strong to protect her, not to bully her; handsome to please her sight, not to torture her wits; rebellious to support her causes, not to offend her logic; imaginative to fly with you, not to get caught in your entangled webs; sensitive to understand her, not to confuse her; determined to lean on you, not to suffer your well-launched attacks; eloquent to appeal to her mind, not to flirt with her friends; charming to give her pride, not shame.

How could you live with yourself? In circles and circles you sent her to fight one lost battle after the other. You exhausted her senses on your swing; one day, she touched the stars in the sky, and the next day she licked the dust off the ground. You played her like a ruthless circus trainer; you gave her sugar when she performed tricks for you, and I could hear her trumpet in agony when your sharp metal hook, with the spiked end, tore through her sensitive skin.

What excuses have you to offer? You told her you were confused and depressed. You said you were a mess from within. You pleaded innocent when you were guilty as charged! Did you not ask for her help? Was it not you who needed her support? Were you not the illegitimate child of receding passion? Have you not suffered the withdrawal symptoms of love? Had she not held your hand through your suffering? Were it not for her ears, who would have listened to you? Were it not for her wise words, who would have consoled you?

Now you sit back and judge her? Now you list her faults and flaws? Now you point a finger at her weakness? Today you turn your back on her? Today you no longer want to be with her? Today she repels you when only yesterday she was never close enough? High time you smashed her wise head with your stupid words? Tomorrow you will wake up and forget all about her, and about all your crimes against her? What a pig! What a drag! What a narcissistic jerk!

Good riddance.

***

100 'Good Girl' Tips in Egypt

Introduction: The Good Girl in Marketing Terms

Your vision:
To be perceived as a good girl at all times.

Your mission:
To bend over backwards to please others.

Your positioning statement:
The Ultimate Denying Experience (apologies to BMW).

Your target audience:
Vain ladies and gentlemen serving vain ladies and gentlemen (apologies to Ritz-Carlton).

Your objectives:
Trial and, hopefully, purchase.

Your marketing mix:
Product: You.
Price: Your Life.
Place: 'Good girl' outlets through 'good girl' distribution channels.
Promotion: Personal ads, word of mouth, favorable reviews, crisis management strategies, cute emails and regular SMSs to all eligible bachelors and mothers of potential bachelors, and last but not least, promote your cooking, sewing, and budgeting competitive advantages in all outings.

Chapter 1 – The Dull Doll Look
1. Have a wardrobe of cute girly, or tom-boyish outfits for family visits – they will never notice you growing up!

2. Have a stash of sexy tops to go with your hidden ultra low rise jeans for hanging out purposes – great disguise!

3. Curly hair is a sign of wildness; straighten it to give you an innocent look or cover it for the ultimate trustworthy look.

4. If you add a few blonde streaks, always make it sound like the stupid hairdresser's mistake.

5. Use lip gloss and pout.

6. Use volumizing mascara and flutter your lashes.

7. Try natural color blush to give you the needed flush.

8. Invest in a great brand of concealer to hide your pores, your age, and your imperfections.

9. Gaze into an imaginary line behind whoever you are talking to for a super dull look.

10. If you are tempted to straighten your back and show off your femininity, remember that you are a heap of bones wrapped up in fat and covered with flawed skin.

Chapter 2 – Watch Your Manners

1. Speak in a low, decent tone regardless of how low and indecent your words are.

2. Laughing out loud in public is not becoming of a 'good girl'.

3. Keep your legs closed and close to one another in public.

4. If you do otherwise, with your legs, in private, always say it is the first time.

5. Smile at all times – it makes you look authentic.

6. Avoiding eye contact does not make you a liar, it just makes you shy.

7. Learn from Halle Berry; the look but don't touch attitude flies well.

8. A 'good girl' never ever smokes – in the bathroom is fine.

9. Shishas and lollipops are out of the question – 'good guys' are quite imaginative.

10. Table manners dictate that you should eat in silence and smile when necessary.

Chapter 3 – The Epitome of Innocence

1. Avoid talking to guys – if possible.
2. Talk to them while standing up – to give the impression that it is a casual chat.
3. Sit with a guy in groups only – you are a 'good girl', remember that.
4. Never get involved with a guy.
5. Hide it if you do.
6. Lie about it if you are asked.
7. Deny it forever when it is over.
8. Never hold hands in public.
9. Do anything you want in private.
10. No matter what, you are always a virgin and you do not know how babies are made.

Chapter 4 – The Sisters

1. Always be seen in the company of other 'good girls'.
2. Never tell a 'good girl' a secret; she will blackmail you.
3. Never introduce a 'good girl' to a potential guy; she will innocently hit on him.
4. Never cry in front of a 'good girl'; she will bring it up again to hurt you.
5. Never talk to a 'good girl' who is turning into a 'bad girl'.
6. Be a diplomat; anything you say will be used against you.
7. Be a nun; forgive, forget, and never tell.
8. Be an idiot; nerds never threatened anyone.
9. If you have an urge to talk about sex, it is never you; it is always about 'one of those girls'.
10. Never call another 'good girl' a bad name to her face – you can say anything you want behind her back.

Chapter 5 – Your Opinions

1. Have no opinions whatsoever.
2. If you have an opinion, keep it to yourself.
3. If you happen to have brains, hide them –brains scare 'good guys'.

4. Go with the flow; if they hate miniskirts, then you've never seen one.
5. Thinking is bad for your health.
6. If you really truly have to disagree, agree first.
7. No matter what, avoid having any opinions on sex, religion, politics, independence, women, men, life, and death.
8. "I aim to please" – repeat it and act upon it.
9. You've always wanted to get married to a guy like your dad.
10. You've always wanted to be like your mother when you grew up.

Chapter 6 – Your Character
1. Have no character; be as colorless as possible.
2. 'Good girls' are modest; stifle your self-esteem.
3. Be soft and mild to attract a 'good guy'
4. You are obedient to the bone.
5. Have no aspirations; you were born to be a mother and a wife.
6. If you have aspirations; they are family Obligations, not your choice.
7. Public displays and private affairs should be kept miles apart.
8. You have a selective version of. Alzheimer's – use it when cornered.
9. Being elusive will make you more desirable.
10. Being a double-faced hypocrite will make you more mysterious.

Chapter 7 – Your Career
1. The sole purpose of working is to meet Mr. Right.
2. Avoid careers; 'good guys' do not appreciate them.
3. Get a job that gives you minimum exposure and zero fulfillment.
4. A promotion is not an achievement; finding a man is.
5. A trip abroad is never good news.
6. Be a friend to all.
7. 'Good girls' do not talk to their male colleagues.
8. If you have to talk to them, make it strictly professional.
9. Your male boss and colleagues are werewolves in disguise.

10. Your female boss and colleagues are always jealous – poor you!

Chapter 8 – Your Weapons
1. Tears will get you out of absolutely anything.
2. Apologies will erase any opinion you might have accidentally voiced.
3. Blindfolds; put them on and rest in peace.
4. Mouth gags are a great tool to keep your mouth shut when hurt and if insulted.
5. Your back; turn it to anyone who needs help and you will never get in trouble.
6. Put on a sad face and you will always be the adorable center of attention.
7. Put on the lost princess look and a savior is bound to show up.
8. White lies were created to make you prettier.
9. Black lies were created to make your man happier.
10. A veil will give you immunity – put it on and do as you please.

Chapter 9 – Absolute NOs
1. Drinking is totally unacceptable – it is always your first sip.
2. Girls with a tattoo are bad – have yours in a hidden place.
3. Girls with a belly piercing are loose –hide yours, but talk about it.
4. You always have a curfew – it is always the first time you've missed it.
5. Dancing is for 'bad girls', 'good girls' stare and curl their lips.
6. 'Good girls' never go to bars or pubs –it is always your first time.
7. Love? Every man you meet is your first, and last, love!
8. Sex? What sex?
9. Internet dating; a 'good girl' always rises above such obscenities.
10. Strength, brains, independence, career, and a life are male-repellents.

Chapter 10 – The 'Good Guy' You Deserve

1. As long as he comes home in the end, he can do as he pleases.

2. As long as he feeds you, keep your mouth shut.

3. He can force you to stay home – you never had a career anyway.

4. He can boss you around – you never had an opinion, so why complain now?

5. He can be as disrespectful as he wants, and you can cry as much as you want.

6. He can beat you up for every white lie he discovers.

7. He is fully entitled to isolate you from the female friends you never had.

8. A 'good guy' is jealous; you will never get to wear your stashed wardrobe.

9. He will never tarnish your innocence and take you dancing; he will have a girlfriend to escort him.

10. If you give birth to a baby girl, he will make sure she is brought up as a 'good girl'!

***

In my Pocahontas nighty, with a whole bar of chocolate stuffed in my mouth and empty wrappers all around me, I watched Nicole Kidman's and Will Ferrell's Bewitched. I needed a distraction. I wanted to give my mind a break. It should have been a nice funny romantic chick flick movie but I found myself drifting away from the main plot and the sub plots, and sinking into a plot of my own; I drew a parallel line between the witch, Nicole Kidman, as Isabel Bigelow, and my humble self – *Don't laugh! I am not talking looks wise! I outgrew that illusion a few years back!*

Let me show you how I ingeniously came to that conclusion: the first thing that got my attention was Isabel's taste in men. She fell in love with Will Ferrell, playing Jack Wyatt, at first sight. Why? Because he was a mess! He even spelt it out for her: "I am a mess. I am a jerk, number one, extremely arrogant, and I love to bleach my hair out." I thought I was the only girl on earth with self-destructive tendencies, bad taste in guys, and a shallow streak! – *I thought wrong!*

A few minutes later in the movie, Isabel could not stand the thought of not telling her beloved Jack that she was a witch! She did not want to trick him into loving her; she wanted him to love her for who she really was. *Sounds painfully familiar!* She struggled with her fear, put her strength together, and blurted it out in his face: "Guess what? I'm a witch!" she said, and what did she get in return? Sarcasm! "Guess what? I'm a Clippers fan!" Jack replied! Poor Isabel was left with the only choice of having to demonstrate her powers. *I do that too!*

His laughter stopped. His face changed. He finally realized that she was a broom-flying, spell-casting, cauldron-brewing witch! Like a lot of guys out there, Jack could not handle her supernatural gift. Behind Isabel's angelic face and frail figure, lay a witch! In fifteenth century Europe, and for centuries to follow, witch hunts involving moral panic and hysterical masses resulted in tens of thousands of executions. The thought of having a witch in town evoked superstitious fear, not to mention dating one or, even worse, getting married to one.

Over the centuries, ignorant masses killed anyone suspected of witchcraft, and labeled the gifted as quacks and frauds. People who failed to comprehend, and accept, the differences that witches brought to the table found it easier to drown, hang, stone, or execute them. The poor witches were alienated in their exile, and eventually, the whole species became extinct and the commoners lived in peace. Books say that witch hunts ended in the eighteenth century. *Oh! Did they?*

I guess not! Today, Egyptian women who have brains, character, and experience are treated the same way witches were treated in the dark ages. Girls, like me, who ask questions and who insist on being honest and straightforward are castaways in this patriarchal society. As human beings, we are inclined to reject people who differ from us; different in how they look, how they talk, and how they think. Watching Isabel's witch-effect on Jack brought back instantaneous memories of my very own witch-effect on men.

Flying and crashing seems to be a pattern in my relationships; I am a relationships expert and I advise people on their love lives, but when it comes to me, my men, and my love life, I am totally clueless. After the initial click, I stupidly, yet willingly, decide to put aside my spells, charms, amulets, and witchcraft. I leave my flying broom at home, get out of my human cloak, and I reveal the real witch within. I express myself with a cursed clarity that leaves no room for confusion or speculation. I share my writings along with my dreams. I show the different dimensions of my character. *I wish there was a delete button in real life!*

In my relationships, I turn into a cute kangaroo that is trying to walk gracefully in a china shop. But alas! With the first step in the shop, I intimidate the owner, who reaches out for his gun. A few more steps and I begin breaking his antique rules. And by the time I reach him, he is totally panicked and freaked out. He aims the gun at me. I plead. He looks me in the eye. My eyes water. He orders me to get out before I create any more damage. I beg him not to fear me. He pulls the trigger. I get hurt. Witch or no witch, I bleed like normal human beings, I feel the pain, and I moan in agony; *a moan that he cannot hear!*

In the movie, Jack realized that his love for Isabel was bigger and stronger than his fear of her being a witch. He followed her home, only to catch her before she took off on her broom. The happy lovers reunited and lived happily ever after. This is the part that I never got to experience. Once a witch, always a witch! People will always hunt me down and try to get rid of my evil influence. They will stone me with their cruel words and ruthless judgments, drown me in negligence and guilt, hang me on the altar of ignorance, point a finger at my scars, and deprive me of true love.

Now I am a witch in hiding; here now on this page I vow to never ever reveal my true nature before a living soul. Like my fellow witches, I will lead a double life. Yes! I have been defeated, but how much rejection can a witch handle? From now onwards, I will lie about the past, cheat in the present, hide in the future. Yes! I have given up, but how much longer was I supposed to fight? I will master the art of nodding, bowing, and smiling and, forever, I will relinquish the rebel that made a home in my soul. No ... No ... I can't ... okay ... one more round ... just one more! I just hope that you are real – *and handsome* – I just hope that you can handle the witch-effect!

***

I was half deaf by the time I got home; I played the music so loud in the vain hope of silencing the voices in my head. I raced every car on the road, hoping that my car would be faster than the thoughts racing through my mind. Today, I discovered a new dimension of the word 'turmoil'; that word never felt as lively as it feels now. I cannot say that I am hurt; I did not get to know him that well or that long. I am just angry; this time my anger is airbrushed with violence. I wanted to slap him; I could feel my hand coming from way behind my ear, my palm pushing against the fine particles of air, my slap landing on his face with all the power I had in me, and I could hear the sound of the explosion as my fingers left their mark on his face. I wanted to hurt him, to shake him, to throw him off guard, just as he did to me. As he dropped me off, I jumped out of his car before I did something to regret. I got in my car, and flashes of our conversation struck me like glimpses of lightening. A silent scream escaped my soul and a frozen tear lay still between my eyelids. I was gasping for air.

Is he a bad guy? Not at all! He is a nice and sweet man who managed to put me in words; he formulated the intricacies, contradictions, sudden turns, dead ends, and blocked roads of my dark maze - the maze that has confused the most avid explorers. Then he encouraged me to 'just be me', expressed his sadness that I filtered my words before they fell into his lap, and gave me all the assuring verbal and non-verbal signs. I landed my heavy loads on him, his face changed, his mind took over, and his heart stopped beating for me. He told me that he wished I were his wife but this - my maze - was too advanced for him. I watched the spark die in his eyes and I felt his soul distancing me. The master of the word was lost for words. Uncomfortable silence, courteous smiles, and small talk added to the heavy feeling of loss - my worst fears.

No matter how sugar-coated it might be, rejection hurts. It's ironic how that 'emotional void' keeps drawing me within; the deep hole gets deeper with every failed relationship or unfulfilled fantasy. There is no way I could reach into myself and fill it with sand, dust, or love. Most women would fill it with food - stuff your tummy hoping that your heart would be full too. It is like an ulcer that eats off your flesh, digs a hole in your guts, and hurts where you cannot heal. Raging voices from the deep void in the center of my body blurred my vision and my thoughts. I sat still but my crucible was boiling and the rotten steam of my burning guts filled my senses.

Were I in his shoes, I would have probably done the same. I understand his logic and comprehend his reasons. In me, he saw the incarnation of the devil - a cute seductress who would replace his faith by an insatiable need for adrenaline. After all, I am the master of mind games! I am eternally grateful for self-control, pride, and willpower. I gracefully backed off by offering my friendship and announcing that I would take a few steps back. Restlessness was crawling on me, bugs were numbing my mind, and I wanted to be home alone with my cats and my laptop. We were both sorry for the loss of what could have been a great trip in the human psyche. I had something else to be sorry for; I was sorry for being me, for being real, for being a bit above the average girl. Now, at this very moment, I wish I were anyone else but who I am now. What was the drill, again? Oh yes, bottle it up, push it down, shove it beneath, and bury it all in the black box.

***

Today, for no justified reason, I decided to come clean with a new confession: women are like ducks. When I look at women, instead of faces, I see ducks. There are several categories of ducks in my world: wild ducks, stuffed ducks, black ducks, and sitting ducks. There are pure, hybrid, and deformed breeds of ducks ... Let me illustrate to give you a better idea.

Wild ducks are fearless spirits, risk-takers, and trend-setters. On the prairie, they live among beasts, yet are highly respected and well positioned. No one dares pluck their feathers, tame, mold, frame, or domesticate them. Those creatures are often criticized, rejected, and resisted but it never makes them any weaker or milder. Whether other ducks look up to them or look down on them, they just cannot be as wild or as free. Unlike black ducks, they know who they are, what they want, and where they want to go. Wild ducks end up on a plate only if shot dead or ambushed.

At the other extreme, black ducks are outcasts; like their market value, their self-esteem and their social acceptance are low. Their flaw could be related to their physique, social disposition, spiritual inclination, tarnished reputation, or unheard-of ideas. Black ducks are sentenced to a lifetime of isolation and alienation – and it hurts them. A black duck wants to be unnoticed, unheard, unseen, and, in a way, invisible. They are the geeks, the nerds, and the pimple-faced teenagers who never grow into anything more assertive. Since the men of this world are not blessed with insight into their souls, black ducks, end up alone or on the plate of an equal male outcast. Being a black duck is a stigma that neither time nor blood can erase.

Going down the ladder, stuffed ducks are a delight to look at and a pleasure to feast over. They are perfect for social occasions and for showing-off purposes – each man on the table has a stuffed duck on his plate! Being full of rice, onions, and any leftovers in the fridge, stuffed ducks look bigger and better than other ducks – posh and grand. They lure men by their big, bloated, over-fed, over-exposed, over-stuffed appearance only to give them, instead of nourishing meat, a plate full of constipating legumes. Needless to say, one can only handle that much stuffed fowl. Their mission in life is to look good – and stuffed! Stuffed ducks land on the plate of whoever pays more.

Sitting ducks are pathetically lovely; you can caress them, fondle them, shoot them, cook them, stuff them, or cage them. They are tame, demure, docile, and disciplined. Sitting ducks are anything but confrontational – they will whine, complain, and bitch about something to everyone and anyone but their offender. Sitting ducks have neither flying abilities nor argumentative capabilities; they are an easy catch, a quick dump, and a perfect emotional punching bag. They do not land on a man's plate; they end up in his fridge for use when there is no other food on his table – sitting ducks are always taken for granted and never appreciated.

Our culture encourages sitting ducks, exiles wild ducks, despises black ducks, and craves for stuffed ducks, but pure breeds are rare nowadays; for example, I am a hybrid of wild and black ducks - and that says it all about me. Men drool over the offspring of crossbreeding stuffed ducks and sitting ducks; such ducklings fit all the molds of our patriarchal society. Some men are stupid enough to think that they can turn a wild duck into a sitting duck, or, even worse, turn a black duck into a stuffed duck. The most hazardous type is a mix of wild ducks and stuffed ducks; they think they rule the world.

Continuing the bird analogy, I would classify swans, ostriches, and birds of prey as deformed breeds. Swans are the vain girls who do not practice what they preach; they claim to be on a high ethical pedestal when their feet are in deep mud. Ostriches bury their heads in the sand thinking they have outsmarted everyone, when they are nothing but blind, stupid, and ignorant. They easily point out the flaws in others, and, because their heads are in the sand, they believe that no one can see their flaws. Hawks are a carnivorous strain of women that feed on their own friends and loved ones. They are full of envy, venom, evil, and have zero tolerance and no resilience. Multiple deformities occur but the outcome is a creature that is, at best, disgusting.

***

I resent him now just as much as I loved him then. I hate that feeling. It is bothering me. He is bothering me. It makes me feel weak, bitter, needy, and sick. I decided to let it out once and for all. I am looking now at his picture and I am forcing all the memories that I have blocked to come out: our first meeting and how I was so turned off by his lack of determination and laid-back attitude; our first phone call and how his voice annoyed me; our first outing and why I had no interest in his lame conversation and anecdotes; our first week and how I spared no effort to push him away. My first angry email and how hurt I was. Our first breakup and how I missed him. It is all flowing back into my head now.

I got used to the voice that had once annoyed me. I longed for the words that had never interested me. I needed his presence in my life, regardless of the definition. I settled for friendship and had to listen to his previous escapades, current flings, and future plans with someone who will never be me. Occasionally, I would compile the strength to walk away only to relapse into him again like an incurable addiction to a fatal drug. I tried all the tricks in the book; pros and cons lists, motivational post-its on my mirror, feminist articles, survival songs, chocolates, and other partners. Nothing worked. He knew that he was graciously stepping on my ego. He knew I was insulted and in love. He enjoyed looking at the new addition to his collection of broken-hearted women. In his condescending, patronizing tone, he refused to validate my feelings, and withheld from apologizing.

One day, he was telling me   his friend – about his new amour when all of a sudden my green-eyed monster rose from the ashes and breathed fire in his face. His words literally and physically hurt me. Listening to him talk about the new kid on the block gave me the feeling of hundreds of little bees stinging my shoulder. We hung up that day and never spoke again. I put him, my feelings for him, and all my memories with him in a big box and threw it down the gutters of my deep psyche. That was almost a year ago and I never missed him once since then. I got off the ground, shook the dust off my clothes, straightened my hair, wiped my face, and walked away. If I were to choose a color for that feeling – the feeling of resentment – I would opt for silver. Silver is the color of bullets, knives, swords, scalpels, and all cutting tools. It is the color of chains, cuffs, shackles, and all restraining equipment.

It is the mirror that only reflects your words and actions; it shows you nothing but yourself, your anger, and your resentment. It is the glamorous version of dull grey. It is a color that smells and tastes like rust, and feels and looks like dust. Like a relationship that went belly up, silver has neither a soul nor a core; it is just the mummification of what was once alive. Sparkling ashes are still ashes and gun powder is what is left after a gunshot.

Silver is not a solid color; it is a metal. Metals are cold, sharp, and they expand under heat and tend to shrink in the cold. Like my resentment of him, he is made of silver. He himself is a cutting edge that wounds women who come his way. I am not the only one; they have all been on his rollercoaster.

The ride starts with a lot of anticipation, eagerness, and excitement, and then once it reaches the point where the girl develops any sort of attachment to him, the relationship goes downhill. It deteriorates slowly, painfully, and heavily. He backs off and she plays hide-and-seek with herself; she hides from the resentment and seeks inner peace. She either becomes a face from the past or a trophy among many others. He is a collector.

Seeing his picture or hearing his name evokes the unresolved anger and animosity that I have been harboring against him. Last week his name came up in a casual conversation and I felt the bitter silver-ish taste in my mouth. I was silently fuming as I remembered my bruised ego. I sat there gritting my teeth and trying to smile when I really wanted to scream and yell at whoever dared mention his name in my presence. I tried hard to name ten good things about him and I only thought of one. I tried to push him back into the black box but he was out and the silver ashes were suffocating me; my eyes hurt, my nose itched, and my skin was irritated as I struggled for a breath. I decided to spit the silver ball out of my system. Passively waiting and wishing that time would wash away the silver residue was not working. This is why I ran to my laptop and decided to write one last time about him. I will no longer push my resentment down; I will let it surface and will capture its metallic essence in a tight mesh and throw it away.

I am cured and healed, but what about you my friend? I know he broke your heart. I know you have had a bumpy ride. I know it hurts. I know you want him. I know you hate him. I know how sad you are now. I know his games. I know your pain. I know you are alone. I know that being with him made you feel lonely. I know he is not there. I know he was never there. I know he will never be there. Do not make my mistake. Do not waste your energy on a lifeless person. Do not build your dreams on someone who will not make them come true. Do not look back at someone who does not want to walk forward. Do not let the silver color blind your golden heart. Do not give him another chance to waste. Do not settle for a place in his trophies closet. I am older and I am asking you not to worry ... the sea is full of fish ... bigger, better fish.

***

He has been on my mind for the past few days; I was angry at him again for what he did to me. I met him back in June 1996. I was not 21 yet. I had just got my first job. I was young, naive, and innocent. He was 33, successful, established, and proud. The first time I saw him, my jaw dropped; so tall, so big, so masculine, and so perfumed. I summoned all my courage and put in a lot of effort to speak up and greet him. He looked from above at this little girl whose eyes gave her away, and his game began. I just wanted what every girl I knew back then wanted: marriage.

I bled for many years. He was cursed.

I cursed him. I took my revenge. I avenged my innocence with plenty of experience; I replaced my dreams with nightmares and sent them his way; I lived to kill him; I thrived to see him fail; I had him on his knees begging for forgiveness and I stood tall as I pointed out his flaws. I planted a poison tree and he stole the fruit. The poison ran in his blood for years, killing his career, his relationships, and his heart bit by bit.

On 18 May 2000 I broke up with him for good. I freed myself from his chains after I tied him to a stake of failure and suffering. I left behind a bankrupt, impotent, pathetic loser. I went on a long journey to reconstruct my self-esteem, determination, career, and heart. I moved on and the years went by. The scars were too many to hide and my love life suffered. He kept coming back asking for forgiveness. He wanted to marry me. He wanted to make up for all his crimes. I slammed my doors wide shut in his face. I hated him.

On 26 October 2006 he died.

I got a call from a common friend who told me that he had died of a heart attack the day before. He asked me to forgive him. I cried. I am still crying. I cannot stop crying. Memories are racing in my head. I am remembering things that I wanted to forget - things that I thought I had already forgotten. His obituary is in the paper and everyone who knew us called me; a very draining and exhausting experience. I still cannot stop the memories from flowing. I want to delete the past thirteen years of my life. I do not mind being who I am now; I just do not want to remember how I got here.

I did not think of him dying before me. This was not how it should have happened; I was supposed to go first and the whole world was supposed to grieve. I am not going to the public funeral because there will be a lot of fuss and gossip to follow. I will go to his house – one last time! I am not prepared to walk into that house again. I fear the living room; I fear the painting of a wide yellow field on the wall of the living room; I fear the sofa that I used to sit on; I fear the chair that he used to sit on; I fear the sounds in the kitchen; I fear the smell of the house; I fear the reception door opening and not seeing him walk through it ever again.

In this living room I used to sit nervously, anxiously, or sadly waiting for him; this is where he held my hand the first time, kissed me the first time, hit me the first time, kicked me out of his life the first time, told me he loved me the first time, and many other first times. The last time I was in this house was about two years ago. He had had his first heart attack. He asked me to forgive him. I visited him, but I did not have forgiveness in my heart; I wanted to show him the new me. I wanted to tell him, "I win; you lose." I wished he would vanish; I wished he would be gone forever so as not to ruin another night in my life.

It is funny how I feel now; I am lost! For more than ten years I have been waking up every morning to challenge him. In the beginning this was the only thing that would get me out of bed. I beat him at any game he called his and rubbed it in his face. He was not supposed to die now; I am not done yet showing him who I am and what I have become. I feel that he cheated his way into winning this. He is gone and I feel as though I have no direction.
I do not believe that he is gone. I do not believe that the last thing I said to him was that I wished he was dead. I do not believe that the last time I saw him I wished he would vanish forever. I never thought I would cry that hard. I never thought it would hurt that much. I wish I had the chance to forgive him. I wish I had the chance to free myself for good. I wish I had never planted the

poison tree ... I wish I was not a poison tree ... I wish I did not live inside a poison tree.

Epilogue

Mirror ... mirror on the wall,
Who's the fairest fair of all?
Mirror ... mirror on the wall,
Who's the smartest head of all?
Mirror ... mirror on the wall,
Who's that girl standing tall?
Mirror ... mirror on the wall,
Who's to hold me when I fall?
Mirror ... mirror on the wall,
Why are you not answering my call?

Oh mirror

The lines and the scars you do not hide;
My scattered thoughts you would not guide.
Me myself and I; the gap so wide;
Oh mirror; you make me look inside.
You show me a girl against the tide;
By the rules she would not abide.
Within your frame, a caged spirit am I?
By your name, what voice have I?
Mirror ... mirror on the wall,
She shall never stutter;
With a new voice, words she will utter.
Mirror ... mirror on the wall,
Her fear you shall never show;
Fearless she is to know.

Cruel mirror
Why show me a figure so broken?
Why tell me words unspoken?

So my mirror
Where is the little fat girl that you used to show me?

Where are the frightened eyes that used to look at me?
Is she still hiding her smile with her hand?
Is she still looking for a magic wand?
Oh mirror ... Why can't you lie?

***

Special thanks to

Karim Terouzian for his lovely illustrations and for the cover design.

Egypt's Insight magazine and Nahed Yowakim for giving my writings a home.

Enigma magazine and Amy Mowafy for helping me voice my thoughts when I had no voice.

Campus magazine and Shady Sherif for welcoming my contributions when others feared my ideas.

Samah Hashem and Hadir Selim for being my friends – for better or worse.

Claudia Venturini for supporting whatever idea I came up with.

Everyone who encouraged me to get published.

Everyone who posted a comment on my blog www.marwarakha.com

www.ingramcontent.com/pod-product-compliance
Lightning Source LLC
Chambersburg PA
CBHW020613250626
47154CB00004B/1491